Wanted

BETSY SCHOW

Also by Betsy Schow

The Storymakers Series
Spelled

Wanted

BETSY SCHOW

 sourcebooks
fire

Sourcebooks and the colophon are registered trademarks of Sourcebooks, Inc.

Published by Sourcebooks Fire, an imprint of Sourcebooks, Inc.
P.O. Box 4410, Naperville, Illinois 60567-4410
(630) 961-3900
Fax: (630) 961-2168
www.sourcebooks.com

Library of Congress Cataloging-in-Publication data is on file with the publisher.

Printed and bound in the United States of America.
VP 10 9 8 7 6 5 4 3 2 1

Dedicated to my beta-reading wizard, Jess. And to the wicked and pun-tastic adventures of PB&J. This book wouldn't exist without you guys.

Happily Never After

A nd they all lived happily ever after," I muttered in falsetto. "Yeah, not so much."

I stared at the wanted poster on an ironwood tree in the Sherwood Forest that had my name, Rexi Hood, emblazoned across the bottom.

Being an outlaw, I could deal with—after all, it was sort of a family tradition. No, I took issue with the fact that the illustration above my name featured my red-caped, directionally challenged cousin with her nauseatingly cute, dimpled smile and long, brown, braided hair, rather than my perma-smirk and short, blond spikes.

"I can't believe those troll turds at *Fox and the Hound News*," I grumbled.

Even worse were the charges listed on the bulletin: *Accomplice to Princess Dorthea of Emerald's wishing crimes. Grand treason against the land of Story.*

"Accomplice," I ranted, pacing back and forth in front of the poster, using the bow I'd *borrowed* from Nottingham Pawn to swat at the tall weeds. "They make it sound like I'm her sidekick! I will go on record to anyone who will listen and state that I absolutely, definitely, no way, no how had a blasted thing to do with that. *Dorthea* pixed off the Ever After crowd by making a wish on a cursed star. *She* turned all the rules of fairy tales upside down and scorched everyone's happy endings. I claim zero responsibility for it."

"*No, you can merely claim responsibility for enabling the release of Blanc, the wickedest of witches, who will white-out ALL endings. Both happy and otherwise,*" a voice whispered, dark and cold as a night in the forest during the new moon. "*Well done.*"

"Shut it, grim reaper," I hissed down at my shadow, or rather the disembodied voice that taunted me from it. "Nobody asked you." Princesses and heroines got fairy godmothers or a guardian angel. I got the equivalent of a guardian demon.

Long story. Short version: a potent mix of temporary insanity and guilt made me jump in front of a stormbolt meant for Dorthea. I died in the process. Well, I sorta died, since she used her powers to bring me back to life. Only something followed me back from the underworld. So as usual, my fairy tale sucks. The end.

Except, not really the end I guess, since Chimera Mountain erupted with Dorthea, Kato, Verte, Hydra, and me still in it. The rest of Story's happy endings were still a bit mucked up because of the wish fallout, so now my friends and I were all outlaws, hiding out in Sherwood Forest. Oh, and the equivalent of the devil's wicked stepmother had been free for about a week.

Minor details.

"*Blanc is many things. Never a minor detail,*" my shadow sniped.

"That evil water hag can have a slumber party with the Little Mermaid for all I care. As long as she stays away from me."

"*That's my little hero.*"

"Go to spell, shadow man." In a fit of frustration I nocked an arrow, aiming straight for the cutesy dimple on the poster. "This rots!"

Thwack. My arrow landed dead center—in the tree next to the one I was shooting at.

"*Your aim appears to be what's rotten.*"

"For hex's sake, Morte. Does the King of the Underworld seriously have nothing better to do than—"

The rest of what I was going to say got lost as green specks clouded the edges of my vision. The pendant I wore cracked, emerald streaks flaring throughout the red-orange fire opal.

Morte wasn't the only souvenir from my unplanned vacation to the underworld. When Dorthea brought me back, she used the opal to pour her life magic into me, becoming my tether to the living world. That tether was really more like a chain that now weighs heavily around my neck. It forged a bond that made it so I can sense her, feel her in my head.

All the time.

I'd have loved to sever our connection and smash the hexed gemstone into a giant pile of glitter, except the opal pendant was the only thing keeping me alive. Once again, minor details.

The bond and the opal also made me Dorthea's backup power source. And right now, for some reason, she was tapping into that. Her presence in the back of my mind, which usually felt like a wispy breeze, turned into a raging cyclone. As the crack in the pendant widened, the air was ripped from my lungs, bringing me to my knees.

Why did Dorthea need so much power? The bright-orange swirls from the pendant dimmed along with more of my sight. My vision was completely awash in that awful, inescapable, green light.

Energy leeched out of me. All I wanted to do was lay down and sleep.

"Coming back to see me again so soon?"

Screw that. "I'm not dying today." I forced myself to my feet with a grunt.

I needed to have a few words with the spoiled wench who kept borrowing my life force as if I were a pair of overpriced shoes.

Unlike Hansel and Gretel, I didn't need any moldy bread

crumbs to find my way home. My body seemed to guide itself, like a puppet being pulled by a glittering emerald thread back to its master. With each step, my strength returned and my sight shifted back to normal.

Before long, a thick, twisted wall of ironwood trees stopped my progress. Their branches rustled and bent, while the knots in the center tree's trunk squeezed smaller, as if squinting to get a better view of the intruder. The trees of the forest still retained a piece of the wild magic that had thrown the world of Story into chaos—yet another lasting memento of Dorthea's wish-pocalypse.

"Move," I commanded in a low and growly voice on par with Prince Kato's or one of the overgrown chimera beasts he ruled. Either the tone worked or the trees could see the threat of murder in my eyes.

Pulling up their roots, they shifted to the side, creating an arched path, so I could enter the clearing. A shack towering atop troll-size chicken legs stood in the center of our sanctuary. It belonged to Hydra, the head-swapping witch—and the shack matched the Baba Yaga head she was currently wearing.

As a headhunter, she had quite the collection. It's not the most savory of hobbies, but I filched random things people left behind, so who was I to judge?

Standing at the base of the chicken legs, I looked up and yelled, "Dorthea, get your bejeweled butt down here!"

Silence.

"You know you can't hide. Not from me." I could *feel* her up there.

Still nothing.

Fine, if she wouldn't come down, I would go up the old-fashioned way. Climbing chicken legs wasn't much harder than climbing trees.

I ascended the chicken legs one wrinkly skin fold at a time. My fingerholds must have tickled because the legs shimmied a little, shaking the hut on top. After I passed the knee, the left side buckled slightly, causing the house to tilt danger-ously forward.

A head rolled out the front door like a screaming crystal ball and sailed through a piece of broken porch railing. Wrapping my feet as tight as I could around the chicken legs, I leaned out with both hands to catch Hydra's head before she went *kersplat*. I did so without thinking, because if I had thought, I would have remembered how gross her heads are and waited to see if she bounced.

My right hand grabbed her by the tangled gray web she called hair; my left cradled her gooey neck stump. "Oh, nymph nads. I'm gonna hurk."

"All the king's horses could not have been putting back me I think," Hydra said.

She'd been dropped and rattled around a lot lately, so she was making less sense than usual. I'd long since gotten over the weird of having just a head talk to me, but I would never get over the *ewww*. I couldn't very well drop her now, which meant I was stuck dragging her up the chicken legs with me.

As sure as the three suns, Ethos, Logos, and Pathos, rise and set over the realms of Story, no good deed goes unpunished.

"Hey," I said. "Do you have, like, feeling in your neck and stuff?"

"Is like chill in frosty bites, yes? Vy are asking?"

"Just because," I answered and stuck Hydra's head on the end of my bow with a *glop*. Problem solved.

With just a few more shimmies, and a lot of cursing from Hydra, we arrived at the top.

Dorthea waited on the porch for us. "I'msorryI'msorry I'msorry."

Her prince, Kato, stood next to her, rubbing his temples. "Rexi, I'm handling it," he said over her run-on apology.

"Bite me, beast boy. You can handle this." I took the bow off my back and gave Kato the Hydra on a stick.

Narrowing my eyes, I advanced on the princess who had turned my simple life into chaos. "Someone found us, right? You needed to go all warrior princess, and that's why you had to snack on my life force."

Dorthea gulped, not meeting my gaze, but the tips of her enchantedly flaming hair crackled with green sparks "Well, not exactly." Her eyes shifted to the open door.

I leaned to the side so I could peer in and see what was making her nervous. Even though Hydra's houses changed shape and dimension based on which head she used, some things stayed constant. Normally, shelves filled with her collection of heads and disgustingly slimy spell ingredients she kept alive for freshness lined the walls of her home.

That wasn't the case anymore. Now there were plush carpets, jeweled vases, and a wall-to-wall closet system stuffed with enough shoes for every foot within a hundred-chapter radius.

Verte bounced up and down on a silk-covered bed, the hair on the green-skinned sorceress's wart swaying with the motion. "Just proves you can take the princess out of the palace, but give her a bit o' magic, and you can't keep her from making herself a new one," she said, ending in shrill cackle.

Dorthea winced. "I'm soooo sorry, Rexi. It was an accident. I swear I didn't mean to."

Through our connection, I could feel her regret, the genuine sincerity in her words. And that only torqued me off more. Because she never *meant* to do anything wrong, and yet I always ended up getting scorched.

My fists opened and closed of their own will. I could feel my nostrils flaring like a minotaur's. "You nearly sucked me dry for a *home makeover*?!"

"Storymaker practice got slightly out of hand. I was supposed to be channeling the creation magic to make one object. But I got distracted and started thinking about how much I missed home and Glenda's fall collection…"

I lunged for her throat before she could finish.

Dorthea shrieked and raised both hands to fend me off, emerald flames shooting from her palms. Her eyes grew wide as the flames hit me square in the chest and sent me flying backward into the rotted wood railing.

Looking up as I fell, I saw Kato quickly kiss his princess so he could transform into a flying chimera.

But there wasn't enough time.

I screamed, but there was no one and nothing to catch me except the ground with a force that snapped my spine in half.

Welcome to my story, where, as usual, I get the pointy end of the arrow.

"In death we are all equal... I jest, of course. If that were true, everyone would have their own monuments. Heroes die in greatness. Villains die in infamy. The rest just die."

—*Grimm's Reapers Guide to the Afterlife*

Forget-Me-Knots

While my body lay broken on the ground, my soul traveled back to the underworld of Nome Ore. There was no bright light, tunnel, or chubby, harp-playing baby at the gateway to the world of the erased. In fact…the gateway looked an awful lot like an office.

As usual, I materialized in the dreary, boxy room right in front of a desk that had stacks of paper tall enough that one good sneeze would create a blizzard of pages. The room seemed to double in size each time I died.

This was number four.

"Six," said a voice, slippery and dark as ink.

"Huh?"

"I'm beginning to think you like it here." Morte—Nome King, Grimm Reaper, and part-time shadow stalker—strode through the office door. He buttoned up his rigid topcoat and stepped behind his desk, where he edited out the dead from their stories. "This is the sixth time your soul has come back to interrupt my day."

I tallied my previous deaths in my head, knowing that he'd just eavesdrop on my thoughts anyway. There was the first time, when I jumped in front of the stormbolt the wicked witch Griz hurled at Dorthea. The second death when Chimera Mountain erupted about a half hour later. The third time, an ironwood tree went rogue and skewered me while Dorthea tried to use her Storymaker magic to transform it into an apple tree. And the fourth, well, even without a flesh-and-bone body, my back felt crooked.

Couldn't help but notice Dorthea was a consistent theme in my recurring fatalities, but since I needed her to bring me back, I focused my ire on Morte instead.

"Someone needs to go to nursery rhyme school and learn to count. That's just four."

"Of course, surely I am mistaken. Even the greatest editor can make an error." The tall, angular man adjusted his glasses on the crook of his nose and smiled like a forest python that was still digesting its last meal.

Morte reminded me of a negative imprint of a portrait, paper-white skin with graying teeth, nails, and hair. The worst part was his eyes—black irises with white pupils. I folded my arms and resisted the urge to step back as he stepped forward. The flickering light from the fluorescent glow crystals in the ceiling cast shadows on his bone-pale skin.

"How I wish you could see yourself exactly as I do." He locked gazes with me. Unblinking. Unflinching. Empty. "Or perhaps you already do, more than you are willing to admit."

"I don't know what you're babbling about." I couldn't help it—I turned away to escape those empty, white eyes that reflected nothing. Which was a mistake. Morte had left the door open, giving me a perfectly awful view of Nome Ore's bleak landscape. What at first looked like the rolling hills of the countryside became far more macabre when you looked closer.

The hills were alive, but not with the sound of music. More like moaning. Rather than dirt, the rise and fall of the landscape was built from the mottled, decaying, and sometimes still-moving souls of the Forgotten—the characters who didn't matter, who no one remembered, who were sentenced to slowly fade into recycled ink piles.

"Whatever," I said, shutting the door on the Forgotten and everything else I didn't want to think about—like my graying hands. It freaked me out that my soul existed in the underworld as a faded reflection of myself that could be erased at any moment. "Can we just get on with this already? I've got better places to be. Like anywhere but here."

"Please take a seat." Morte gestured in front of his desk. A petrified Forgotten had been twisted into a chair with literal "arm" rests.

Turns out you don't need a body to shiver. "I'll stand."

"Suit yourself." With a *thunk*, Morte tossed a large book on his desk, sending papers flying.

I barely noticed. I focused on him through the flurry as he thumbed through the *Compendium of Storybook Character*'s glowing, ethereal pages, which held the extensive records of all the lives that mattered. The stories of the characters that would be remembered and retold. Both hero and villain.

Taking an involuntary step back from the daunting book, my foot landed on something with a crunch. I looked down at pulverized powder and the remaining chunks of a blackened, withered hand and fought the urge to hurl.

Morte sighed as the twisted Forgotten chair lost a chunk from the other arm. "They don't make souls as sturdy as they used to."

Sans serif scarabs scuttled out from under Morte's desk to nibble at the pieces of Forgotten. The little punctuation mark bugs swarmed my feet, then ran away as I kicked and stomped.

"Still afraid of a few bugs?" he asked with a *tsk* and snatched a paper from his desk, making a few notes on it with his red-ink laden quill. Rather than a feather, his pen was shaped like a sickle. "I doubt the book will discriminate based on that. A very small flaw in comparison to your many, many others." He tapped a page of the compendium with his sickle. "So tell me, little hero, was your story worthy to be recorded this time?"

Wanted

It wasn't, and he knew it, since he saw everything, lurking and taunting me from my shadow.

The first time I died, I had done so to protect Dorthea, which should have been enough to land my name in those golden pages. But turns out it's hard to scam the *Compendium of Storybook Characters*.

When I took Morte's red sickle and used it to sign the page, I may as well have been using invisible ink. The book soundly refused to acknowledge me. As if it knew that I had sold out my friends to claw and survive my way into a happy ever after of my own. It rejected me, not caring that anybody in my situation would have done the same thing. It didn't matter that, in the end, I tried to make it right.

As usual, I didn't meet someone's—or, in this case, a stupid book's—expectations. I shouldn't care what it thought. I have never wanted to be a hero. Or a villain. Except, if my name and story weren't recorded in the compendium…

Through the closed door, I could still hear a symphony of discordant wailing. A silver serpent slithered out from a hole in the chair-shaped Forgotten. "Traitorsssss like you dessssserve far worsssse."

"That's a Grimmed lie!" I swatted at the snake even though I was unsure if it was real or if I was so screwed up that my conscience was now manifesting as a scaly critter, rather than a self-righteous chirping cricket.

"*Is* it a lie?" Morte tapped his pen on the desk. "You have been here for quite a while this time. Maybe the Girl of

Emerald has realized it was a waste of life magic to resurrect a worthless betrayer like you."

"Dorthea will come."

"Perhaps you're right." Morte extended his arm around me like a creeping vine. "She is a hero after all," he continued. "She's pure and good. So she'll come because it's right. Even though she'd rather not."

"It's not like that. We're friends." My protest sounded hollow even to me. Perhaps part of me wondered the exact same thing.

"You can't hide from me. Don't forget, I see all of you," Morte said, his slim and sickening grin splitting his face. "You don't have friends and only look out for yourself. You push people away so they can't abandon you like your mother did. Then your father—"

Panic blew through me like a storm, knocking away all my defenses. "Stop it! Stop it!" I put my hands over my ears, knowing it would do nothing to keep his voice out. I tried to channel the strength of the forest.

I am a child of the trees. Though the wind may howl, I will not break.

"How many times did you utter those words in the Emerald Palace kitchens, waiting for your father to come back? Face the truth, Rexi," Morte said, bringing the sickle up under my chin. "You were born to be forgotten."

"It's not true. It's not true," I mumbled, still holding my ears and rocking slightly.

Wanted

Find me. I sent the thought to Dorthea like a prayer. My usual fury at her had decayed and crumbled, just like everything else down here. All that was left was the aching need for her to see some worth in me. I'd promise anything she wanted—anything so I didn't become one of the Forgotten. I'd be strong and good and kind and perfect and just.…

A soft, warm, green tendril of flame reached down from the ceiling above me.

Swallowing my moment of weakness, I glared down at the king of shadows. "Well, that's my ride. As always, it's been a ball. Let's not do it again."

I started to reach for the tendril, but Morte pulled a thin, metal, knotted cord from the binding of the compendium and, flicking it like a whip, wrapped it around my neck. Even without a body, the soul can feel pain. I shrieked, and the cord tightened as he yanked, cutting into me, ripping and fraying a place so much deeper than flesh.

"You're not going anywhere yet." He brought his cracked, gray lips next to my ear, close enough that I could feel the breath he shouldn't have had. "A coin for the ferryman or a knot for me—no one leaves the depths of spilled ink without paying the price."

Very carefully, I unwound the knotted wire from around my neck. It wasn't a whip. It was my story line, pathetic and withered as it was. Each knot in the line stored a key part of who I was, everything I had done. If anything happened to it…

"Choose," he said, holding my story line in front of me, the left segment angled up as an offering.

I touched the metal knot closest to me and saw a flash of my story—the moment I gave up my life for Dorthea. "No." I pulled back as if burned. "Not that one." Never that one. It was the only truly good and selfless thing I had ever done. And Morte couldn't have it.

The Nome King harrumphed. "Fine, fine, but hurry up. Surely you don't think you are the only one to die today. With Blanc free, I expect business to pick up in droves any day now."

The green tendril flickered. I could feel Dorthea's exhaustion. She wouldn't be able to hold it too much longer. "This one," I said, blindly touching the next closest knot.

As soon as I grasped the line, the silver knot changed color, tarnishing and growing dark. A memory sprang to life in my mind, like watching a scene on YouMirror, except rather than seeing, I was experiencing the memory. Again.

I felt the heat as if I were back in Chimera Mountain. I tried to let go of the knot, knowing what was coming.

"Too late," Morte said, holding my hand firm to the wiry cord. "Good luck surviving with your mind and soul intact." As he sent me swirling into my past, he whispered, "Take the easy path. Break for me."

"Being right means nothing if no one believes you."

—Chicken Little, *The Day the Sky Fell*

Escape Down Memory Lane

U gh," I groaned, draped atop Kato's broad and fuzzy back in his chimera form. *"Seriously, I feel like I've been run over by a flock of wicked witches."*

"No, just stabbed by one. Be grateful you aren't dead anymore."

I shuddered. I hadn't died. Not really. It was all nightmare— the creepy, skinny man with the white pupils that looked drawn of shadows and charcoal. The mountain of dark, featureless bodies… The book…

"Close your eyes to the truth, you thief. It makes no matter. You still owe me a serious debt, which I'll enjoy collecting, one ink drop at a time."

I reared up. "What did you just say to me?"

Kato pushed me back down with his wing. "Stop squirming. I didn't say anything. No one did."

But I'd heard a whisper. Like someone was in my ear. I must have been hearing things. I'd finally lost it. That was as good an explanation as any for why it felt like Dorthea was next to me, instead of back in the prison chamber with Verte.

"It's hotter than the gingerbread psycho's oven in here," I said, changing the subject. "Isn't there a therma-spell you can turn down?"

Kato jerked to a halt. "You want to walk?" When I didn't answer, he started flying again, skimming the blazing-hot fire flowers. "I didn't think so. This volcano was built and enchanted centuries ago for one purpose: to keep Blanc imprisoned. Griz came within a second of freeing her, so the last defenses must have been triggered as a fail-safe, that's all."

A boulder fell from the ceiling of the grand chamber, shattering and sending pointy obsidian projectiles through the air.

"Safe for who?" I muttered. "Well, hurry and go sing the mountain a nursery rhyme or something to chill it out."

Kato didn't answer, but something else did.

"Our vigil is over," a low voice rumbled.

"The pact is broken," a shriller second voice wailed.

"Blanc is free," a third said flatly. "May Grimm forgive us."

This time the voices weren't just in my head. Kato heard them too.

"No, no, no." He bucked, rolling me semigently off the mismatched shorter white wing that Hydra used as a replacement

for the one Griz had blown off. Flying upward, he perched on his stony throne and bowed to an obsidian chimera that had three heads. "Elders, hear this plea. We defeated the storm witch before she freed her sister. Blanc still rests in her fiery prison. Calm the mountain's fury. Stop this before it's too late."

"It is already too late."

"The White One is loosed."

"Our story has ended."

I really didn't like the sound of that. "Hey, fur ball, what's going on?"

Kato ignored me and spoke only to the elders. "There must be a mistake. I implore you, don't do this." The elders no longer responded. Their heads splintered apart and crashed to the ground.

Kato stared at the pile of rocks that used to be alive, then turned sharply and swooped me up in his black and broken claws. "We have to hurry and get the others."

"What's happeni—?" I broke off, choking on the hot dust in the air.

"The elders set the mountain to erupt to try and keep Blanc contained, with or without us in it."

"That's murder!"

Kato flew with speed and precision, dodging both the falling pillars and the shooting columns of lava. The air had turned smoky and acidic. "Our lives are a small price compared to the hundreds of thousands of stories at stake if Blanc escapes this mountain."

With a boom, part of the tunnels collapsed, cutting us off from the rest of the mountain and our friends.

"Nooo!" Kato howled and frantically ripped at the rocks, while I fell off his back, forgotten. "I have to get to her."

It was obvious who he meant. In that moment, Kato wasn't the guardian of the mountain, concerned about containing evil. He was a prince desperate to protect his princess.

"No one cares about you, little hero," the shadow on the wall, or in my brain, whispered.

A wave of hatred for Dorthea and the rest of the Ever-After Elite rose within me. I could sense Dorthea and knew without a doubt she was safe and protected. No matter what she did or how she screwed up, she was always okay. And like always, I had to scrape, swindle, and steal to survive.

I yanked on Kato's horns to get his attention and turned him to the exit. "They're fine. They're outside." As I said it, I could almost picture it being true.

"What? How do you know?"

When Griz threw that stormbolt, I'd chosen to balance the scales for my sins. My life for Dorthea's. Bringing me back with her magic, Dorthea knocked the scales askew again. I felt the weight of that debt. I felt her.

"You are bound," the shadows rumbled, the mountain rumbling as well. "She owns you."

The mountain continued its angry tantrum around us. "There's no time to explain, and I wouldn't know how anyway." I put a hand on my hip. "You're just going to have to trust me."

Kato growled like, Fat chance, and kept digging.

The heat had tripled—no, quadrupled. No, amped up

exponentially with each passing second. My lungs burned with every breath I took. Kato's bleeding paws didn't look much better.

Love makes people do stupid things.

"Please," I wheezed.

His face twisted in pain, looking from me to the blocked passage. "Grab on quickly."

Pushing off from the ground, Kato began a steep ascent through the peak of the mountain. At the volcano's exit, through haze and the smoke, we could see Dorthea being held by a hovering catterfly.

"Hurry!" she called, frantically waving to us.

"Told ya," I said weakly as my skin blistered and popped. My victory at being right was hollow as the strength left my arms, and I couldn't hold on to Kato's back anymore.

I let go.

Kato screamed my name as the lava rose up to greet me.

"Rexi!" that same voice echoed from outside the memory. "Come back right now."

I wanted to, but Kato was so far away, and I could still feel the lava burning into my bones…

"*Rule #16: Since amnesiatic spells are a preferred weapon of villains everywhere, it's always a good idea to carry illustrated ID. Many a royal has found themselves a serving girl due to this simple oversight.*"

—*Definitive Fairy-Tale Survival Guide, Volume 1*

Waking Ugly

A broken claw scratched my cheek while a growl snapped my soul back into body. "Ashes and iron, Rexi!" Kato said. "Start breathing or so help me…"

Breathing was hard. Maybe because there was a heavy, weeping weight on my chest. I opened my eyes a sliver, just enough to see an ocean of flaming curls sparking against my opal necklace. "For the last time," I wheezed. "Get off me, you pixing cow!"

Dorthea raised her head, a delicate trail of tears on either cheek. Ech. The moron even *cried* beautifully.

She whacked me in the gut less beautifully as she scolded, "Don't scare me like that! You took too long to come to."

With a grunt, Kato rose off his haunches. Including his twisted horns, he was now nearly twice my height and his set of white-and-tan mismatched wings were easily as wide when extended. He wrapped his scaled dragon tail around me and started to pull me to my feet.

"Well, excuse my rudeness," I said, rolling my eyes at Dorthea. "Maybe I wasn't too excited to get back since it's mostly your fault that I've died three times!"

Kato stilled, halting before I was all the way standing. "Rexi," he said quietly, the creases in his brow growing deeper. "You've died six times."

"Ha. Ha." I stood up the rest of the way on my own. "Hilhexing-larious. Make fun of the zombie girl."

"No, really." Even in chimera form, Kato had humanlike expressions. Just fuzzier. And at the moment, his muzzle showed no sign of his teasing.

I turned to the others, who'd gathered around me. Dorthea looked like she might burst into tears again. Hydra was still perched on the bow, which was now stuck in the grass like a head on a pike. Her decrepit forehead wrinkled even further. And Verte stared off into space, the carved emerald eye in her belt growing cloudy.

I chuckled awkwardly, trying to fill the silence. "C'mon, guys. I think I would remember." No one laughed with me. One: storm bolt to the back. Two: tree to the gut. Three: ground to the spine.

I staggered, feeling as if something were trying to pull me

under the soil as I tried to remember more. Kato was by my side, supporting my weight before I fell. On its chain, the bright-green swirl in the opal pendant pulsed and widened slightly, swallowing a piece of the surrounding iridescent red.

Dorthea's emotions welled in me—concern for me as well as a tidal wave of love for Kato. I'd felt this particular combination before, but I couldn't place when.

As Kato looked down at me, I wanted to drown in those borrowed feelings and his wintery-blue eyes.

"*Turning into a swooning maiden, little hero?*" my shadow whispered beneath me.

Morte.

Rejecting the warmth growing in my chest and cheeks, I shoved myself away from the lion-bodied King of Beasts. "I didn't ask for your help, you big mutt. Don't you have to get back to your mountain and toast marsh-spellows over Blanc's prison?"

I thought it was quiet before.

I was wrong.

Even the wind seemed to hold its breath.

"What's wrong?" I asked.

With everyone else so quiet, I couldn't block out the grim chuckling that no one else seemed to hear.

"*You* are wrong. Allow to refresh memory. The vhite empress is running off. This vorld is doomed to kerput. And you seem losing slowly mind." Hydra clucked her tongue. "Any questions?"

Questions? Only enough to fill all the pages of Witchipedia. But I hated all the pitying looks on their faces, like I was Dopey's half-as-smart little sister.

"Oh that." I snorted. "Yeah. I know. Totally just messing with you." I forced a laugh and a smirk, punching Kato in the haunches. "I sure got you good, didn't I? And you," I said, pointing to Dorthea. "Just a little payback for killing me off six times. Make it seven and don't blame me if your gowns magically turn into hammocks."

Dorthea's lips curled, and her hair flared green in disgust. "You are soo—AHHH!"

"Right back atcha," I said, ducking while Kato took a fake swipe at me with his paw.

We were an odd group. My life force was trapped in a necklace, Dorthea's in her hair, and Kato's in his nails. I hadn't noticed until then, but one of his nails was shorter than before I plunged to my death.

Now Kato was down to four claws and I was more indebted than ever.

"So what now?" I asked, tearing my eyes away from Kato.

Answering me with a groan, the earth beneath our feet shifted. Cracks spread out as the magic workshop sprouted from the dirt. Like an ill-omened weed, it popped up randomly and obnoxiously from time to time. On each occasion, a bit more of the structure seemed to have been eaten by the earth. I refused to go inside anymore since the building wouldn't even pass the three little pigs' building code. The current workshop was two and a half walls of mossy stone and about half of a thatched roof—unless you counted the giant hole as a skylight.

A small, slimy, green worm inched its way out of the workshop. It stared at us with large eyes magnified by thick glasses that wiggled a bit as it chewed on a meal of paper.

"Oh, get on with it already, you old meddler." Verte's eyes refocused and narrowed on the bibliobug, but her belt's eye remained cloudy.

At the sorceress's prompting, the creature flickered and transformed back into an old man with untamed salt-and-pepper hair. As he tried to spit out the wad of paper cud, it got stuck in his mustache. He sure didn't come off as an all-supreme magical being. But I could feel his power thrum through me, similar to Dorthea's—but stronger. The Storymaker of Oz. One of the beings responsible for writing everyone's fate.

I shook my head. The Storymaker of Oz was a lie. A fable taught to children to help them sleep at night. An excuse to absolve the wicked of their sins. One look at my story was all the proof I needed that nobody was looking out for me but me.

Oz was a Story*faker* if you asked me.

But chock-full of magical goodness to protect us all the same.

Oz was supposed to be training Dorthea to be Maker's apprentice, so she could fix all the rules of magic and get her parents back. Part of that meant harnessing the Emerald curse to work with creation magic. I didn't think it was going so well since she kept killing me with it.

My back flared again in pain at the thought. "What are you doing here?"

Dorthea might have gasped at my lack of respect, but Oz only tilted his head to the side, like a cat watching will-o'-the-wisps. "I'm intrigued to see what you'll do."

"You're the all-powerful whatever Oz, so haven't you already written that part? What are we all doing sitting and playing magic tutor if the biggest bad is on the loose? In fact, tell me again why you don't just grab a pen, lock Blanc back up, and give us all unicorn rides while you're at it."

"Rexi!" Dorthea yelled, her hands glowing green.

"That's enough," Kato roared at us both.

The old man fluffed his moth-eaten, oversize, tweed jacket. "It's just Frank now, not Oz. This story is no longer in my hands, and I swore not to meddle and just advise." He ignored Verte's disgruntled snort and continued. "My Storymaking days have passed."

"Very convenient," I muttered. *Storyfaker*, I added silently because I didn't want Dorthea to zap me. "Then how about you advise already? It's been..." I wasn't sure how long it had been anymore, so I ignored that part. "Where's the gloomy 'the end' you've been moaning about?"

At that, Oz snapped to attention and focused his stare on me—no, more like *through* me. "That battle is coming, I assure you. Blanc is dangerous because she doesn't make the same mistakes other villains do. She won't face you head-on until the last possible moment. She's not hiding. She's growing her strength while she lets other pawns do the work for her."

"I'm no one's pawn," I ground out, keeping the sour taste at the back of my throat.

Dorthea reached out to touch my arm but pulled back as green flames licked the edges of her fingers when she got close. With a sigh, she rubbed her temple. There were dark circles under her eyes that weren't there before I died this last time.

I sensed her blasted concern again, and it only made me feel worse.

Shrugging, I looked away. "Whatever. Sorry dying puts me in a foul mood."

Kato bridged the gap between us and wrapped his wings around both Dorthea's and my shoulders. "Fair enough, hearth sister, but remember this: there is a very fine line between strength and stupidity. Don't confuse the two."

The aim of Kato's barbed comment was much better than mine with an arrow. His words hit me right in the heart.

Folding his wings back, he turned to Dorthea. "Now, my lady, if you don't mind, since I have no more need to fly anywhere, I'd just as soon get back to human form." A smile crept over her face as Dorthea nodded, taking his furry muzzle in her hands.

I looked away.

At first, the magical malfunction of the "true love's kiss" rule had been pretty funny to watch. But after a dozen smooches that switched the enchanted prince back and forth between his forms, I was ever after over the show.

Dorthea's feelings swelled in my chest again, all warm and gooshy. Even with my eyes closed, I had a very clear mental picture of the dark and handsome boy whose auburn hair had grown just long enough to cover the little horned nubs he retained even in human form.

I could hear Dorthea whisper, "Hey, you."

"Hey back," Kato answered in his human voice, still almost a purr.

Like the rest of us weren't even there.

Ech.

Love turned people into utter morons. I didn't need what they had. Didn't want it. I'd figure out the minimum I needed to do to trick the *Compendium of Storybook Characters* into accepting me. Who cared how many times I'd come back from the dead? This time would be the last, and that's what mattered. I'd get it right this time so I could live a long and *uneventful* ever after.

Morte was a problem though, and my thoughts circled back to my plotline, the number of dark knots slowly growing in number compared to my untarnished ones. How much of myself had I already forgotten? What would happen if the entire line went black?

"*Rexi will cease to exist,*" both my shadow and Verte answered in an eerie tandem. "*Long live the king.*"

"Organization Tip #3: A place for everything and everything in its place. A tidy torture chamber is far more inviting than a sloppy cell. Just because you're imprisoning someone doesn't mean it can't be pleasant."

—Better Castles and Dungeons

You've Got Male

S peaking up!" Hydra said, her head starting to slip off the tip of the bow.

Verte blinked, her eyes regaining focus. The emerald eye in her belt did the same, winking away its cloudiness. "What are you on about? I didn't say nothing. You're getting senile, you old bat."

"Sharper than old, green goat."

The two bickered back and forth while Oz tried to referee—or more specifically tried to stop Verte from kicking Hydra's head like a goal between the chicken legs.

Their cranky "look at the harmless ancient hag" routine didn't fool me for a bit. After years of indentured servitude in the Emerald palace kitchens, I knew one of Verte's prophecies when I heard one. And this foreshadowing made my feet itch to run as far—and as fast—from here as I possibly could.

"*That is one of the few talents you do possess.*"

"Grimm, would you mud your mouth already?!" I shouted at Morte, forgetting no one else could hear him.

"Who do you think you're sassing?" Verte pointed her sharp, poppy-red fingernail at me while the smell of burned bread and magic filled the air. "One set of frog legs fricker fracker coming right up."

Remembering the last toad-ally awful evening she'd given me, I took a leaping dive for the grass, a tinkle of bells ringing behind me.

tinkle tinkle "You've got mail." *tinkle tinkle*

Verte's spell flew over my head.

"You've got m-*ribbit*."

After rolling onto my back, I looked to where I had been standing. A hot-pink toad with shimmering wings and a messenger pouch hovered there, spitting out ribbit-laced profanities unfit for translating.

I snickered. "Way to turn fair-e-mail into a fairy fail."

Verte harrumphed and stared indignantly. "Bah. Shows what you know. I clear as murk altered the directional fizzics of my spell to stop the intruder."

"I would be impressed if I thought you could react that fast. However"—Oz plucked the fairy frog out of the air by its wings—"right now I am more interested in what this message is and how it managed to find us here."

And when Oz said "interested," that is precisely what he meant. Not excited. Not concerned. Merely engrossed in the puzzles and paradoxes that seemed to sprout up around us. Including him. The old crank made me twitchy. Oz was twice the trouble of that princess-obsessed Mimicman and half as nice to look at.

Oz tried to take the pouch off the frog, who croaked in protest, shooting out its tongue, which got snarled on the Maker's mustache, startling him enough to drop the message. The fairy frog flittered about Oz's facial hair in a sparkly, sneezy cloud of dust.

Picking up the miniature messenger pouch, I squinted so I could read the *To* line. "G. Pendragon. So is it a wrong address?"

Hydra's face paled to match her hair. "Ach, nyet."

Verte's green complexion also dimmed, going from a dark moss to princess pea soup. "Spells bells. Anything but that."

I racked my brain going through all of Fairy Tale's families. The surname was familiar, but it wasn't coming to me. Who knows what other chunks of memory I'd sacrificed to Morte?

Oz stroked his mustache, seemingly forgetting that the toad was attached to it, despite the angry ribbits. "There are few wizards powerful enough to charm a fair-e-mail across Myth and into Fairy Tales. But only one wizard is left who'd actually want to talk to her. Good luck. You'll need it."

Puzzle solved, his curiosity waned, so he poofed himself

into a fist-size, horned rhimouserous and scampered off into his workshop.

Immediately after, the building shrank back into the ground, the cracks knitting back together as if they had never been there.

"Coward," Verte said with a tsk.

"Do I want to know the *her* Oz referred to?" Without waiting for an answer, I held the message as far from me as possible. If the useless Storyfaker wanted nothing to do with it, then surely I didn't either.

"Ooh, is it a love letter? The suspense is killing me." Dorthea took the pouch off my finger, then yelped trying to open it.

The fairy frog beat its wings together at Tinker Bell speed. It darted away like a pink, slimy, mutant humdinger bird, with ribbits that sounded suspiciously like laughter.

Verte swiped the letter and bonked Dorthea on the head with it for good measure. "You newt-brained ninny. What sort of big shot wizard would send a message that any nosy princess could read? Good thing that Merl has a wee bit of a cauldron problem"—she brought her hand to her lips and mimed drinking—"or else he might have remembered to add a self-destruct spell."

"Yeah, lucky me." Dorthea shook out her injured hand and stared after the rapidly disappearing winged frog. "I don't imagine it's good for anyone to know where we are. Will you go after her?" Dorthea asked Kato.

He'd been human for all of two minutes, but still Kato

grinned (all too eagerly in my opinion) and spun Dorthea dramatically into his arms as he puckered up.

I groaned. "Hey, Tweedle Ditz and Tweedle Dumb. Anyone else think that, I don't know, maybe sending the furry beast that's on wanted posters all over the forest is a really bad idea?" I held my hand up.

Verte raised her hand and cackled. Hydra made a few gagging sounds, which I was counting as a solid vote in agreement.

"Besides." I squinted and pointed to the frog sitting atop of the tallest ironwood. "Everyone knows that fair-e-mail messengers don't get paid until the letter is delivered to the actual recipient. She's not going anywhere."

Verte tapped the wart on her crooked nose. "Glad one of ya still has the sense Grimm gave you." She walked over to Hydra and knocked the bow with her foot. "Well, Rexi, per the usual criminal patterns, you have a new toy, so you musta made it to the pawn shop. Did ya get what we ordered?"

I took out the small, brown box from my pack and handed it to her. "Yeah, I got it." Though it felt like it had been days rather than hours since my brief trip into Nottingham.

"Good, we gots a letter to read." Verte conferred in nonsense babble with Hydra. Once that was done, the sorceress handed out orders. "Dot, you and your thief buddy need to go get a chest out of the attic. It's next to the other unspeakable things."

I didn't budge, because I had already seen the gizzards, lizards, oozing eyeballs, and carnivorous houseplants that

Hydra kept in her pantry. I *really* didn't want to know what "unspeakable things" she kept in the attic.

Sensing my reluctance, Verte sighed and her face softened, making her look like a sweet old lady. Which made me want to say, *Oh, Grandma, what big teeth you have…*

"Or perhaps Hydra would be a dear and get it? Oh, I forgot she can't. Some thieving traitor led the giant Tinman to the rainbow where he kersquished her body."

Hydra managed to summon a single, sparkling tear. Apparently she was as skilled at guilt trips as she was at swapping heads.

Dorthea didn't look too excited to do the errand either. "Wouldn't it be better if Kato went?"

"Why no, it pos-o-tutely wouldn't. Now go and take the enchant-alator."

I peered around the chicken leg to where Verte pointed and saw a shimmery glitter tube spiraling upward. "No one could have told me about the enchant-alator *before* I climbed those scrawny drumsticks?"

"No time. Git."

I did have to begrudgingly admit, the enchanta-lator was a nice addition. Dorthea and I rode up in silence, the green flaming tips of her hair sparked and hissed, speaking volumes.

"What?" I asked. Though if I really focused, I could have used our bond to see what she wanted.

"I'm worried about you."

"Stop using my life like it's a credit card you order shoes with and quit murdering me. That'd be a solid start."

Dorthea stared down her nose at me. "I said I was sorry, okay. But that's not what I meant."

I sighed. "Let me guess. That mumbo dumbo pix about ceasing to exist that Verte spouted." And Morte. I was worried about it too, but since no one knew about my grim reaper… "I don't want to talk about it."

"Of course you don't, but we're going to anyway."

"Because you command it, *Your Highness*?" I said with a fake bow, my tone lower and rough like sandpaper.

"No, because I'm your friend and I care about you and I'll keep bringing it up until you deal." Dorthea huffed, her flaming hair flared brief but blindingly. "What was that? Did your shadow just move on its own? That's crazy."

"Yes, you are. I'm glad you finally noticed." The tube dinged at the top of the chicken hut just in time. I stepped out hastily to put some distance between us. "Let's just find the chest and get out of here. This place creeps me out." The creaky wooden attic had more cobwebs than walls. And I was pretty sure I saw fangs on the dust bunnies that were flitting in the dark corners.

Dorthea had obviously stopped short with her makeover before she hit the attic. Good thing, since it would have sucked my life force dry. And I'm not entirely certain I could come back from that. Before she'd made the wish that broke the world to pieces, I'd been privy to the other servants' gossip in the Emerald Palace for six years. I'd thought the Emerald curse was just a bunch of hooey the king and queen concocted to excuse keeping their daughter locked up.

Yeah…not so much.

Girl of Emerald, no man can tame. Burn down the World, consumed by flames.

A prophecy, a threat, a promise—who knew? The source of her magic, the green flames that lived inside her, that danced on the tips of her hair, that leaped to her hands at the barest spike of her temper—it was hungry, always looking for more energy. And I was the most readily available snack.

Whack.

Something hit me in the back of the head.

"Are you even listening to me?" Dorthea said, shoe still in hand.

"Nope."

Apparently she'd been talking, but I've gotten pretty good at tuning out voices lately.

"Ugh," she said, stamping her other heel. "Why do you keep pushing me away? I'm trying to help you, glam it!"

"Yeah, I can tell," I muttered and rubbed my head. "Look, I know I screwed up," I said, turning to her and clasping the opal necklace. "Right here's the proof. The debt I can't ever steal enough to pay off. You own my life and my deaths. So for the love of Grimm, just give me some space and stop making it worse."

"I never wanted this," Dorthea said quietly, her voice

shaking. "You've changed. I'd make it all go away if I could. I wish—"

"Don't even think it," I cut her off. The w-word was strictly off-limits for her. Not even Oz really understood her powers and what she was capable of.

I scanned the room for what we'd come here for. Just under the north window rested a medium-size chest that looked like it had been carved from the warped heart of an ironwood tree. That by itself would have made the chest unbreakable, but the container was also wrapped with chains and a half dozen padlocks.

Whatever was in there was worse than poison-apple-level bad news.

Dorthea must have thought the same thing, cuz she shut up the second she saw it. I took a deep breath. As long as the chest stayed sealed, I was safe. Probably.

We carried it to the enchant-alator and went down in it silently, each of us holding a side. We set the wooden chest down on the grass just as the third sun was setting behind the trees.

"Good. There's one half. Now for the other." Verte motioned to Kato, who dropped a pill in a bucket of water.

Nothing happened immediately, but Kato stepped back anyway and took cover. Hydra opened her mouth, but he cut her off with what we all already knew she was about to say: "I know. I know. Wait for it."

The water bubbled, just a few tiny plops at first, but within seconds, it came to a full boil. With a sploosh, two big feet burst out from the bottom of the pail. From there, legs emerged. The bucket was just the right size to cover the lower half of the torso that grew out the top. Then two manly arms popped out the sides. And last, a head—with a blindingly white smile and a mass of blond, curly locks that would make Goldy scream in jealousy.

"This isn't right. We didn't order Grow-A-Beau." Verte checked the box again. "Where's the spellphone? Somebody call customer service."

"Hello, gorgeous," I said and took a step closer to inspect the boy in the bucket. Just to make sure it was safe.

"Rexi!" Verte yelled. "This is your fault. I know it."

"Rex," the Grow-A-Beau said slowly, as if testing his own voice. He stared deeply into my eyes, then winked and flexed his muscles.

Hydra whistled low. "Hot toasted borscht."

"Glammed right," Dorthea said, nodding. At Kato's growl, she hastily added, "If you go for that sort of thing."

The ironwood chest began to shake, the lid pushing and rattling against the chains.

"Oy. Now we've done it." Verte's chin hair curled and spun wildly. "She smells fresh meat."

6

Rotten to the Core

She?" I squeaked and pointed to the chest. "What's in there?"

"Man-eater," Hydra slurred.

Verte clucked, "That was never proven." The chest thumped, like someone was trying to get out. "I know you don't like Gwennie, but you gotta swap heads with the hussy since only she can read the message."

Dorthea went over to inspect the newly grown hottie. "So if the Gwennie head is in the box, isn't swapping into it gonna be a little tough, since, I don't know, the body we just grew is a guy and he kinda already has a head?"

"Off wiff 'is head," Hydra slurred.

"Ew, no," I said, vetoing the idea.

"I don't see why not." Verte ignored me and skimmed the small print on the package. "Blah, blah, blah, blah, brain not included. Well, obviously, since who needs their eye candy to think." She looked up and shrugged. "Might work."

"No!" Dorthea and Kato shouted together.

"Why can't she just zap her soul from one head to the other? Why do we need a new body at all?" I asked.

"To make the transfer successfully, the new head gots to be connected to a heart. Without that anchor, the head rots and loses connection to Hydra's soul," Verte said.

"Bah," Hydra said and rolled her eyes. The left one popped out of the socket and plopped on the ground.

I covered my mouth to stop the chunks of my lunch from escaping.

"See," Verte said, grabbing the eye and popping it back in Hydra's head. "We're lucky she's lasted this long."

Dorthea put her hands on her hips. "Well, that body is defective merchandise. Just call the shop and make them deliver a new one. Duh." Spoken like a true shopaholic.

"We could do that," Verte seemed to consider. "And at the same time, we place a sign with one of those thingeramoggoos that tells everyone in Story, *We are here*. Next idea."

"She is half-right," Kato said, defending his princess. "We just need to exchange the body. It's getting dark, so the forest won't be safe to navigate. I'll go to the shop in the morning. Surely the message can wait until then."

Hydra burped. "Being excused."

"She needs to swap outta this head before it spoils any more. For that, we need a new body. Rexi will go," Verte said without even looking at me.

"It's too dangerous and there are too many traps," Dorthea said, backing up her fiancé.

The Emerald Sorceress overruled the princess. "Rexi can do it." It wasn't that Verte had faith in me particularly, but she was the one who made the deal for me to work off Dad's taxes in the palace kitchens. Only she knew exactly who I was and why I could avoid the traps laid in these woods.

"Nope. No. I absolutely forbid it." Dorthea crossed her arms over her chest.

"*She doesn't believe in you...*"

I didn't need Morte taunting me from my sunset-stretched shadow. I could feel fear and hesitation from Dorthea's leaking emotions.

Beyond that, it bothered me that everyone was talking about me as if I weren't there. Like I didn't have a say. Nobody cared what I thought because my opinion didn't matter.

"*Precious that you think a puppet gets to decide which way its strings are pulled.*"

I knew exactly what I needed to do.

"Verte's right. I'll go," I said.

There was cursing, arguing, eyelash batting, and more cursing, but eventually Dorthea agreed. And by the time night fell, I made all the necessary preparations. I was ready.

Dorthea and Kato escorted me to the opening of the clearing. Verte and Hydra were nowhere to be seen. Better that way, really.

"Be careful," Dorthea said. Her flaming hair acted like a torch, lighting our surroundings. "Stay out of sight. Don't talk to strangers. Go straight to the shop and back, mind you, and don't steal anything you don't absolutely have to."

"You sound like your mother," I muttered, rolling my eyes. Kato squeezed Dorthea's hand, snuffing out the green flames glowing in her palms. I could feel her worry flare along with her agitation at me.

Her glare said plenty too. "I mean it. You could have *at least* let me give you a disguise makeover. We are all outlaws."

"No way in spell am I letting you touch me with your Maker magic. Besides, I'm a hexed sidekick; nobody's looking for me. And if they were, my wanted picture doesn't even look like me. For once, being unimportant has been useful."

Kato stepped forward and squeezed my shoulder, then pulled me close to whisper in my ear. "Just because you have a fool's luck doesn't mean you should act like one. Be smart and come home to us."

I shrugged him off and backed away with a chuckle. "You two are the ones the world should worry about." I stared intently at my fidgety hands. "So take care of each other. And…stuff." As far as good-byes went, that was as gushy as I could handle or offer without tipping them off that I had no intention of coming back at all. I turned to the handsome and dimpled golem and gestured toward the path. "Well, let's go, DumBeau." (He'd earned his name due to lack of brain and the fact that his ears hadn't really stopped growing.)

He followed me, smiling blindly and brightly, without a care for what was happening or that he was defective goods. At least he no longer wore a bucket around his waist. Kato had dressed him in some clothes from the Huntsman fashion line that Dorthea had accidently conjured using her Maker magic.

But there ain't nothing free in this world. Magic always has a cost. To get anything of value, something of equal worth must be sacrificed. Equivalent exchange. It's been my experience that royals do most of the getting, while the rest of us do the sacrificing. And while I was packing provisions for the journey, I discovered that Dorthea's little magical shopping spree for DumBeau had swiped nearly all of Hydra's spell ingredients, as well as most everything I owned. In fact, I was pretty sure that DumBeau's calf-length coat was made of mossy loam from the forest and leather from my last good pair of breeches.

Which is why I felt no guilt in taking his coat. Repossession.

I waited until the ironwood tree sentinels closed the archway behind us before trying it on. Since I was shorter, the hunter's coat swamped me a bit. But the soft moss hood was large enough to keep my face concealed.

"Rex?" DumBeau said with his head tilted to the left.

"Hate to break it to you, but you're not actually going

anywhere, so you don't need it anyway." I pulled out laces I'd swiped from a ridiculous pair of leafy riding boots. With heels, of course. I'd found them when I was scavenging for useful supplies in the home makeover disaster.

Knotting the laces together, I made a long rope and fastened him to the nearest tree.

Securing my knots tight, I took a step back. DumBeau's smile was gone, his lower lip sticking out as if in deep thought, which was extra difficult without a brain.

"Look, it's nothing personal." Aside from bungling my name, DumBeau was quiet, good-looking, and compliant— the perfect man. Much better than that fur ball prince. "Sorry, but running away is sort of a solo project."

In my defense, I'd only said I would *go*. I hadn't said where or with whom. Or to do what. Or that I was coming back. I'd just agreed that I could make it through the merry men's traps. If everyone assumed something else…well, that wasn't my problem.

I turned away, making myself ignore the pitiful, "Rex," since I already felt enough guilt misleading the others. I didn't need to add someone else's disappointment. Tracing the tree line, I scanned for where I'd stashed the bow (after Hydra had been taken off it) and hidden my pack, the one I'd crammed with enough supplies that it would have been a dead giveaway that I wasn't planning a quick store run in the middle of the blasted night.

"It's all about survival," I reasoned to myself. As long as I stayed in the clearing, smothered by the bond, waiting to die again, trying to be good enough for Dorthea, Kato, and the rest of them—for the compendium—my life would never be my own. I would be no better than DumBeau. How long before my "friends" were arguing if I was more useful without my head?

I took a deep breath, adjusted the supplies on my back, and started walking. It was done. They were better off without me. And I was gonna be better off without them. As for DumBeau, when I didn't come back, Kato or someone else in the group would go looking and find him in the morning. Probably.

"Rex."

Or sooner.

Verte stood directly in my path, holding the Grow-A-Beau by the rope I'd tied around him like a leash. "Well, it looks like you done gone and swiped everything you could carry, but I think you forgot something."

Being caught escaping brought back some unpleasant memories that Morte hadn't confiscated. One in particular, from just after I'd turned twelve, when I broke into the Emerald Palace and boosted a certain gem dragon to prove my worth to the gang. Swiping the gem hadn't been a problem, but even now, six years later, I needed to work on my exit strategy.

I froze. "Look, I can explain."

"Don't bother." In the dark of the forest, Verte looked like a shadow, dimly lit by the soft glow of the carved eye in her belt. I felt like it was glaring at me. "I'm surprised you didn't try to run off sooner."

"Look, you have to let me—"

"Save yer bebuggered energy," she interrupted. "I'm not gonna stop you."

"You're not?"

"Nah," she said, stepping forward, DumBeau's leash in one hand, a ball of slime in the other. "I've done did all I could for you. It's time we see if it was enough."

"What do you mean?" I asked.

"You'll know when you know."

Yep. Clear as mud.

"Great, well, good luck with the whole 'end of the world' thing." I pulled the straps on my pack tighter and moved to walk past her.

"Said you could go. Didn't say I was done with ya." She put out a hand, and her red, pointy fingernail stopped me in my tracks. "You were given to me to pay off a debt. Do one last thing and you will have paid in full."

"Define 'thing,'" I said carefully.

Morte had called me a puppet, and I could feel those strings tightening, forcing me to dance to Verte's tune.

"If Hydra doesn't have a new body to finish the swap by morning, her essence will decay with the head she's in." It was then I saw what the gurgling puddle of slime in Verte's other hand really was.

Wanted

It was Hydra.

Or what was left of the Baba Yaga head.

"How you do it is up to you." Verte handed me the end of DumBeau's leash, which brightened his face immediately. He looked at me with adoration, and even though it was probably the result of some love spell for the first thing he laid eyes on… I knew I couldn't do it.

"I'm not cutting off his head—and you can't take mine either." I added the last part for good measure.

"Didn't expect you to, and if we're gonna have a chance of surviving the switch with Gwennie, she's gonna want a body with curves more like that bow you done stoled." Verte moved her hands in arch then and wrinkled her nose at me. "An' arrows got more curves than you and Dimples."

Relief at not being decapitated warred with being offended at being called flat chested. I was going to have to break into Nottingham Pawn and get the right body this time. But if I brought it back, I'd have to explain to Dorthea that I was leaving again. For good. She'd either get all gushy and beg me to stay, or suck me dry. It depended on the day.

A speck of glitter rained down with a ribbit, landing on my nose, and gave me an idea.

"It's not enough to be evil for evil's sake. The best villains always have a strong *why*—or at least a very tragic backstory that makes them understandably criminally insane."

—*Seven Habits of Highly Evil People*

Sense of Dred

No good deed…" I mumbled and picked myself off the forest floor after tripping for the fifteenth or sixteenth time. The ironwoods still had a bit of that chaotic wish in them, and they seemed to be pulling up roots to catch us on purpose. Behind me, the lead line had become taut. DumBeau struggled, thrashed, and snagged on something.

Pulling the newly grown hot dope on a rope tied around his waist was taking three times longer than it should have. Bad enough that I was rusty when it came to spotting traps set by the merry morons of the Sherwood Forest, but even when I found a safe trail, the brain-impaired DumBeau kept walking into tree trunks.

It was so tempting to leave him to whatever fate had planned. But the thought of abandoning someone in the forest, even someone not technically a person—I couldn't put my finger on it, but it made my stomach feel like it was being eaten by night crawlers.

That and he made an excellent pack mule, carrying all my supplies.

"Mrmph," he mumbled my name with his lips pressed against the ironwood he'd just collided with.

I sighed and started back to help.

A twig snapped and a horse whinnied.

I dropped the leash and took to the trees. Sure, maybe I was being paranoid, but that doesn't mean there weren't all manner of wicked whatevers waiting to haul me up a beanstalk or feed me some sort of poisoned fruit or vegetable.

No sooner had I perched on a branch than a man called out, "Who goest there?"

I knew the voice wasn't Morte's; he hadn't whispered to me since the last sun went down. And this voice was rich and full. The sound carried like it owned the air. A rogue or crusty bandit perhaps?

My gaze was drawn first to the glint off the ax he carried on his back, then his figure. The rider was dressed in dark leathers with hair like ebony wood. I couldn't see his face from my squirrel's eye view, so I couldn't guess his age, but given his size, he was certainly a man, full grown. He jumped off his horse so he could examine DumBeau.

"Ho there," he said and picked up the end of the leash.

DumBeau didn't answer, so he couldn't give me up. The tree, however...

Though they were still creepy at night, Verte and Oz had bespelled the ironwoods so they were no longer murderous. Usually. Unfortunately, this one took issue with having me up its branches, so it shook me loose. I landed solidly on the stranger. Making a quick decision, I acted as if I'd meant to ambush him all along, grabbing his ax and pressing it against throat.

"Who are you are and what do you want?"

Up close, I could see the man was not a crusty bandit, as I'd first guessed. Or near as old. Rather, he was a young man who had a few years on me and a few notches of rugged gorgeousness on DumBeau. A rush of tingles spread through my chest and a niggle of recognition wiggled into the back of mind.

Which was stupid. How do you recognize someone you've never met?

His dark eyes burned like coals as he said, "For sport, I shall give thee ten seconds to yield. Then, all bats are off." Aside from butchering the cliché, his words were formal without an ounce of familiarity or concern that I was straddling him, trying to shave the stubble off his chin with his own ax.

"It's bets. All *bets* are off. Are you pixed in the head?"

"Nine. Ten." Before he even finished saying the number, he bucked his hips, twisted, and, just like that, our positions were reversed. "I confess to being new to these phrases, and thus have no knowledge of this *pixed*, but I believe you, young huntsman, mayhap be."

I gulped and closed my eyes, ready to meet Morte for the whatever-th time, but the weight on my chest disappeared as quickly as it came. When I opened my eyes, he was climbing back on his horse, his ax already in place upon his back.

"You're not gonna kill me?"

"Time runs short while the grail quest goes long. And despite my reputation, I prefer not to slay lads still unblooded."

The words popped out before I could clamp my mouth shut. "Lad? You must be blinder than all three mice, and you talk like you have a stick up your—"

"Button your lips, boy, or you shan't keep them." The rider huffed. "Now, go before I change mine mind."

Run, moron, the smart part of my brain screamed. Normally I would have agreed and been well on my way. Who he was, why he felt familiar, or where he was going—so not my problem. But something about this guy rubbed me the wrong way. Or maybe playing the part of a huntsman was going to my head.

It was easy to be brave when I knew, if worse came to worse, my deaths were only temporary.

Nocking an arrow, I stood in front of the stranger's horse. "Maybe you've got an ogre earwax problem, so I'll ask again: Who are you are, and what do you want?"

Tilting his head, the guy pulled the reins to make his horse stamp her feet. As she did, bright flames flicked down her mane and tail. Her eyes flared red, the mark of a night mare. Her hooves smoldered and steamed, coming close to crushing my feet.

"Rex," DumBeau blurted in a higher pitch. I'd almost say he sounded concerned.

Join the club.

"Rex, huh? A very noble name to live up to. Aye, you might be amusingly brave, I'll grant, for such a small lad who can't even hold a bow proper."

I fell for it and checked my stance while the rider chewed the side of his lip, keeping it from turning up into a smile. "The grass is green on both sides of the fence, so as I have your name, boy, you might as well have mine. Mordred. *Hiya*," he yelled and spurred his horse, galloping away.

I froze. Unable to correct his rotten turn of phrase. Unable to bark about being mistaken for a boy. Unable to do anything.

The name along with his weird speech finally made me recall why the surname Pendragon was familiar. The "Merl" Verte mentioned must have been short for Merlin. The man-hungry head "Gwennie" short for Gwenevere.

Kato and Dorthea were from the land of Fairy Tales and wouldn't know. But I was a child of the forest that separated Myth and Fairy Tales. And these trees were steeped in legends.

But legends were called that for a reason—because they were stories that had already been penned into the compendium, passed down from a different age.

My father used to sit in these treetops with me and tell of

how the ironwoods of the Sherwood Forest came to be—born from a battle that littered the forest with blades and blood. A battle where Mordred, the young dark prince, the traitor, the usurper, was killed.

The moon moved out from behind a cloud, and as its light shone down and cast a shadow behind me, Morte's inky voice whispered, "*You should know best of all, little hero. Not all who die stay dead.*"

"*Rule #9: Dysfunctional families are a cornerstone of fairy tales. If you want to be a happy ever after, it's imperative that you get an evil stepparent. If your parents are perfect, try getting cursed by an evil fairy and raised by strangers.*"

—*Definitive Fairy-Tale Survival Guide, Volume 1*

8

Hoodwinked

I wanted no part of this. I was ready to run as far and fast as I could in the vain hope I could get clear of whatever had brought back Arthur's bane. But before I could leave these woods forever, I had one last task to perform for the House of Emerald.

In my experience, rich men became that way because they miserly lorded over their treasures, or they took whatever they wanted to replenish their stores. The Pawnbroker of Nottingham was both, apparently.

This late, I expected him to be fast asleep—just not in the back of his own shop, wearing velvet jammies and drooling on a pile of glittering inventory that would make Aladdin squeal in delight. Pressing my nose to the window, I could just make out some of the open boxes on a nearby table. They said things like "Recall," "Expired," and "Sample: Not for Individual Sale." There were also brand-new, plain, brown boxes nearby for the old goods to be repackaged in.

"Well, that explains your defectiveness," I said as DumBeau bumped into my back. Including lack of brains, he seemed to have a personal space issue. This was particularly problematic since his ears now stuck out about as far as his shoulders, whacking things as he went by. "There's no way I can sneak you in there without waking up the Shyster of Rottingham. So you are getting doorbell ditched."

Just without the doorbell part, I thought and tied his leash to one of the posts supporting the roof. I took my pack off him and laid it by the exit in case I needed to make a hasty getaway.

After reaching into the bag, I felt around for something suitable to pick the lock. I had bread crumbs, an ivory comb with wiry hairs stuck in its teeth, a little black dog figurine I'd swiped from Kato, and my newest addition—a pewter button that had *fallen off* Mordred's ax holder. Finally, I found one of Dot's hairpins.

Something sharp bit into my finger. I pulled out the fairy frog messenger with a little squeeze to keep it from biting me again. First I'd get in, then I'd rely on the fairy frog to get the body out.

Charming that you think it will be so simple, little hero.

With a quick suck of breath, I shoved the frog into the

pocket of my Hunstman coat and knelt down in front of the locked door. I tried to remember all the things the Sherwood thieves' guild had taught me while I was growing up—details far more useful, in my opinion, than Dorthea's junk lessons on princess slaps and manners.

"First jam the pick to the upper left," I said quietly to myself. I didn't make it to the next step because the door swung open under that slight pressure. No, I wasn't that good. The broker had left the door ajar. Odd for a guy who felt the need to outfit his front perimeter with guarding gnomes. But they'd all been asleep too.

Ugh. I had a bad feeling this was going to end like the palace heist. That door had also opened with ease. How could I have known that blasted emerald dragon would come to life and start shrieking like a milkmaid when I swiped it?

I shook my head. No. This time would be different. In and out. And while the pawnbroker and his snoring were somewhat intimidating, he was no Verte. Thank Grimm she was one of a moldy kind.

Going slowly, I pushed open the door enough to slip inside, ready to scram in case the bolts creaked. Silent as the swan princess, not wanting to linger, I went straight for the shelf labeled "Miracle Grows."

Near the sole lit candle, a capsule in a vial lay out in the open. No box. No label. I kept looking for one that I could be sure would be the right fit, but the unlabeled vial *may* have ended up in my pocket. I couldn't really say. It was dark, and I was busy skimming the ones with boxes.

Grow a Pet. Grow a Heart. Grow a Conscience. Grow a Pair. Ah…Grow a Body. This time I picked the box that had the actual picture on it instead of the cheapo stuff. I couldn't remember which model I was supposed to grab though.

"Eh. Anything would be an improvement over the last one," I mumbled, thinking about the lumpy, humpbacked body Hydra used to have. I reached into the coat pocket and pulled out the fairy frog, pinching its lips before it started ribbit cursing me. "You wanna get paid, don't you?" It stopped trying to glitter bomb me, so I took that as a yes. "Then fairy-ferry this back as fast as you possibly can." I used the ribbon to tie the box to the flying frog and pitched it out the door for a head start.

And with that, my debt to the House of Emerald was paid. I was free.

"*A pawn is never really free.*"

I blew out the candle on the shelf, effectively banishing Morte and my shadow with it. "Now, just one last thing." I pulled the bow and arrows off my back and blindly felt around for the empty corner.

I had a soft spot for unwanted things, so I usually only took small trinkets that had been discarded or that no one would miss. I don't know what had possessed me to take the bow earlier. Homesickness caused by temporary insanity of repeatedly croaking probably. But I had no need for them.

62

As Mordred'd pointed out, I wasn't good with a bow; I'd been lousy at archery growing up, despite practicing until my fingers bled. And the years in the palace kitchens had made me handy with a knife but had done zero for my bow work. With a sigh, I placed the bow set back where I'd borrowed it from.

"Now, this is a first. You've got some raw talent, boy, but the basic tenet of thieving is *taking* rather than returning."

Not the bald, fat shopkeeper—his voice had been harsh and grating. Not Morte or Mordred either. The voice behind me had a musical quality, a rise and fall that charmed the ears. A sound that made you think of a rakish smile and the warm autumn sun. Or it used to. Now hearing it so unexpectedly, it snuck into my soul, as crafty as the man it belonged to and, just as quick, shred it to pieces.

"C'mon, boy. I don't have all day. Turn around careful like, with no sudden movements."

Don't do it, those broken pieces of my soul screamed. *Run. Never look back. Never let them see you cry.*

Except I was literally in a corner. There was nowhere to run.

I am a child of the trees. Though the wind may howl, I will not break, I reassured myself.

Plastering a mask on my face, I turned and smirked at Robin Hood.

"Long time no see, Dad."

The prince of thieves stared at me for a good thirty seconds before recognition lit up and widened his moss-green eyes.

"Rexi?!" he whisper shouted, all signs of composure abandoned.

Breaking his cool soothed some of my cracks like poultice.

I am a child of the trees. Though the wind may howl, I will not break. Not for you. Never for you.

"Eyesight failing you a bit, old man? Or maybe you never thought you'd see me again after you sold me off to that moldy green hag?"

He stepped back, putting his hands up in front of him. "Shhh. It wasn't like that."

"Oh, it wasn't?" I railed. "Maybe your memory is as warped as mine, but I can't imagine another scenario where the master of thieves forgot to steal back his own daughter. I was there. I saw you. You came, then you used me to pay off taxes and left me to rot in Emerald!"

Anger and yelling wasn't stealth, but it was either that or dissolve into tears.

I'd rather die for real.

The pawnbroker snorted loudly and jerked, knocking over some of his goods before settling down again.

"Did I teach you nothing?" Dad set his crossbow to the side and grabbed a coin purse from a hidden compartment under the till. "Your whining can wait until we're done here."

Wrong thing to say.

"Oh, spell no—"

Dad stopped retreating and rushed me, putting his hands over my mouth. I did the only sensible thing. I bit him.

At that point, a lot of things happened at once. Dad yowled. DumBeau came crashing through the door, bringing the support beam I'd attached his leash to with him. The racket snapped the pawnbroker to attention. He grabbed one of his stock of Excalibur knockoffs and came lumbering toward us much faster than his girth suggested he was capable of, especially with a portion of the roof raining down around him.

"Now, look at what you've done. Haven't changed a bit, I see," Dad said, breaking into a run—but not before grabbing what he could on the way out.

"Me?" I said, sprinting faster, passing him. "Here's a news flash. Your debt is paid in full and your daughter died. So from now on, pretend you don't know me."

We made it outside while the pawnbroker picked his way through the debris. Dad snagged my hood and yanked, pulling me to him in a crushing embrace.

"Hey. Get off."

That only made him hold tighter.

"Stupid, willful child. I never thought I'd see you again. This isn't over. I'll lead him away and meet you at the tree house." He trailed off, then reached low and tossed me straight up into the air as if I weighed less than a leaf.

Swallowing a shriek, I grabbed a branch and hung on, taking shelter in the trees as Dad bolted into the forest, the pawnbroker chasing after him.

"Newly Reduced Price: The perfect cookie-cutter home for anyone with a sweet tooth. Plenty of upgrades, but needs a new oven. Motivated sellers. MUST SEE!"

—Rumpel's Real Estate Brokers

9

Home Decrepit Home

I bit my lip, half to stop it from trembling and half to stop from screaming curses after my father. Like one hug and leading the fat baldy away would make up for leaving me for SIX YEARS?! He could go to rot for all I cared. I didn't need his approval. His love.

"Argh. Do you hear me? I don't need you!" I scoffed at him even though he was out of earshot. "You must be snorting pixie dust if you think I'm gonna fall for this again. That I'll go wait for you *not* to come back for me."

And yet, as soon as it was safe to jump down from my hiding place, my feet still headed to the treetops I'd grown up in rather than taking the fastest way out of the woods and back to the land of Fairy Tales. "The merry men's camp is sort of on the way," I rationalized.

In the same way that if you kept turning left, you'd eventually go right.

My footsteps started off slow, but soon they quickened, maxing out my speed. I raced back to the home of my youth, hoping that maybe just this once....

A smile split my face even as my nerves and the jogging made my tummy roil. What would Will and Tuck say when they saw me after so long? Had they wondered where I'd gone? I'd never managed to be one of the boys, but they'd tolerated me while I tried.

Fryer Tuck in particular took care of me when the guys' relentless teasing proved too much. We'd kept vigil over the campfires and grills together, and Tuck had taught me the subtle art of revenge: spitting or putting boogers in Will's food.

The skill proved quite useful in the Emerald kitchens.

For years, I'd kept most of my merry girl memories locked tight in a corner of my mind, but I freed them now. I could hear my childhood giggles in the rustling of the leaves. I could feel the thrill of climbing trees and leaping from branch to branch like a flying squirrel. I was better at it than any other—even if I always came up short in the archery and looting departments. Sure, I could swipe all manner of little, broken, discarded trinkets, but that didn't pay the bribes or the taxes.

Still, I'd proudly bring Dad all the old pots and slipped horseshoes I'd found in the forest. He'd sigh and pat my head, then send me off to Tuck to fry up some food while he went back out to rob from the rich and give to the poor. And given that we lived in trees, there really wasn't anyone poorer than us.

But it had been a good life, and I missed it fiercely when I was in a soft bed during my Emerald imprisonment. A daring thought darted through my head. Perhaps this was where my story was supposed to go, now that I was free of that Emerald nonsense. I didn't need a new life; I could just go back to my old one—my pre-Dorthea life.

The idea was fragile and shattered the moment I got within view of the encampment. There were no campfires, none of the raucous merriment that had given the gang its name. Ladders still hung from the trees, but the vines were tattered and rotted through. Pieces of the tree house's boards lay scattered around the forest floor. The trees themselves were twisted; some looked like they were snarling, with their branches reaching high into the sky as if cursing it. Others bent low, almost as if they were weeping. The only things living here were wingding bats. They mocked me from their perches with their red, shining, beady eyes.

Anger toward Dorthea surged through me, and for a moment, I tried to pretend that she was to blame. Her carelessness had thrown the entire magics of Story in disarray, had brought the trees to life, had broken all the rules of Fairy

Tales, so wasn't it possible that her wish had ravaged this place? But even I'm not that good of a liar. The smell of decay alone told me that the forest had reclaimed this little piece of land from the merry men a long time ago. I doubt Dad had been here for years. Or that he was ever coming back, for that matter.

Hope is so much crueler than terror or fear. I despised myself for allowing it to sneak back under my defenses.

Kato was right—I was a fool.

"*Fool's errand indeed.*"

I hated hearing Morte, yet a shot of adrenaline coursed through me as my shadow grew again from the light cast from a lantern nearby. A branch snapped near the light. Even as I looked, I knew better, knew it wouldn't be him.

Grimm, I hated being so cynical. Yet I hated being right even more.

Mordred stood near the lake, holding the lantern and reins as if he'd just watered his horse. He dropped both of them in favor of his ax when he saw me.

"Oh hex, really?" I said to the universe that was bringing royals back into life just to pix me over.

A frown tugged on the lips of the legendary dark prince. "Nay, I am not a practitioner and have not a spell, but an ax to blind. Explain fast why you follow me or meet it up close."

"You have a talent of being too literal, and I have an epically bad talent of being at the wrong place at the wrong time." I rolled my eyes and threw my arms out. "Come here and get it over with already."

"*Eager to see me again, little hero?*" Morte said in a deep, mocking lilt. "*I'm flattered.*"

"You wish, Mr. Tall, Dark, and Demented."

Mordred's frown deepened, and though he had been coming toward me, he stopped. Perhaps he was unsure if it was fair to slice open a crazy person. Normally I'd encourage that sort of thinking, but I had a plan. Ish.

I needed him to come forward…oh…about four more feet. I also needed the trap Will and Tuck had laid there to still be active.

"Are you speaking to me, lad?"

I sighed, having second thoughts about leading someone so dense into a trap.

He took a slow step and leaned forward, examining me up and down again. "You have an unusually high-pitched voice and are fair of face. If ye were naught as flat as a scabbard, I'd think thee a maiden."

Second thoughts gone.

"Iron and ashes," I swore, trying to mimic Kato's curse and gravelly tone. "I never thought to see the dark prince simper like a damsel."

That did it. His hesitant steps lengthened to a purposeful stride.

Three. Four.

Snap.

A vise sprung up from the ground and closed around Mordred's foot. The mechanism had a rope trailing off it, and the springs were tight, yet not sharp. No more than a nuisance, really.

"Twill take more than this," Mordred growled and raised his ax, ready to hack at the rope.

I whistled high and sharp to stop him. "I wouldn't do that." I pointed to the rest of the trap. The one that would fire a poisoned arrow a second after the rope went slack.

He altered the course of his ax right as it brushed against the first strand of rope. "A devious trick."

"Eh. All's fair in disdain and war."

He furrowed his brow. "That is not how the saying goes, I believe."

"Duh."

His jaw ticked back and forth. I couldn't tell if he was fighting a begrudging smile or grinding his teeth. "Dare I hope that there be a way to disarm such foul trickery?"

I sat down on a nearby rock. "Feel free to hope, but if you want my help, there's a price."

His eyes narrowed. "A goodly man and noble hero would never demand ransom to spare a life."

I could only imagine that my grin looked as wicked as it felt. "Who said I was a hero?"

"Rule #32: If perchance you run afoul of wolf or bear, never fear. Hold on to your cape and help yourself to a wee snack and wait for a huntsman to come to the rescue."

—*Definitive Fairy-Tale Survival Guide,*
Volume 3: Enchanted Forests

10

Wet Behind the Ears

I expected him to hurl curses or maybe even his ax at me. I didn't expect deep, rumbly laughter that echoed through the forest like thunder.

"I suppose it was too much to hope that someone like you wouldst be a naive charlatan aspiring to become one of the great knights of legend."

"What do you mean 'someone like me'?" I folded my arms, trying to hide the discomfort his statement gave me.

"'Twas meant as a compliment. So-called heroes are oft martyrs with flawed ideals who sacrifice themselves and take their followers with them. I can't abide such idiocy."

I snorted and rolled my eyes. "So says the villain of his

story. I know who you are. I know you killed Arthur and died trying to take his throne." I watched Mordred's face set into hard lines. But he didn't dispute what I'd said.

"The ends justify being mean."

The means, I thought but didn't poke him further. Every tense muscle in his body was battle worn and screamed trouble. I could have, should have, left him. He was smart and agile enough, he might have been able to get out of the trap unharmed—mostly. And if he didn't make it, not my problem. He likely deserved it. But if he really was the Mordred from legend, he'd already been entered into the compendium. Despite that, he was standing before me, and he was death impaired, like me.

I couldn't go back to Dorthea. Dad had abandoned me again. I had been delusional if I'd thought being away from the House of Emerald meant I could get clear of Morte's shadow. Verte's prophecy rang in my ears. *Rexi will cease to exist.* The feeling of slowly losing my memories and myself to Morte…

I needed to be free from everything that bound me, and I was starting to be far less picky about how I got there. "If you want me to disarm the trap, tell me how you came back to life and why."

"Then I suppose my blood shall run twice upon this ground, as I cannot tell you what I don't know."

I bent down and flicked the trap rope menacingly. "Nice try."

"Truth is truth. Thou hast the upper hand, so a wise man

would tell all he knows. All I can do is tell mine story and let it be judged if it be worthy." He waited. Watching me.

I huffed and crossed my arms. "Fine, but I don't have all night. And try talking normal. Your wordy drivel makes my brain hurt."

"As thou…you wish."

I grimaced at the w-word but waved him on.

"I remember being cut down in an open field by this very lake. I'd never held the grail, so I couldn't undo what had been done. At least I could close mine eyes with the satisfaction that I had stopped Arthur's tyranny. 'Twas enough. When my eyes opened again, there were great giants of trees surrounding me. My body was sore, as if it had not moved for ages."

He looked at the biggest tree, once the greatest ironwood of the forest. Dad had called it Camlan. The first tree. The marker where Arthur and Mordred fell. But the great tree that I'd spent so much time playing hide-and-seek in was very nearly bare and ready to topple over.

Still staring, Mordred blinked several times and held his head, as if he was trying to focus on something. "There's a remembrance, but it's fuzzy and hides from mine sight. Though I cannot recall much of my past and know little of this new world, I am the son of the Avalon mists, and I can feel the balance of magic is in unrest. One thing I know is war… I can feel it coming, lad. My sword calls to me, and I will answer."

While someone else might scoff at his sudden amnesia, I could guess the cause of it, given our mutual state of rebirth.

"Do not pick at what you cannot understand, little hero. Send him back to me and begin earning your place in the book."

I ignored Morte and warily stepped closer to Mordred, staying well out of arm's reach. "Let's say you're right, that there's bad stuff coming. Whose side are you on? Blanc's or Dorthea's?"

"I know not either of these names." He spoke so quietly I had to lean in to hear. With a tilt of his head, he smirked and whipped the underside of his ax around my waist, drawing me closer. "There is but one side. Mine."

Before I had time to react, he'd cut off the vise. I had but a moment to grab the rope and renew the tension. As I steadied the rope, he backed away.

"I'm sorry, Rex, but I can't allow anything or anyone to get in the way of my quest to reclaim my throne and the grail. I hope your friends come back soon to disarm the trap. Or that your grip is stronger than you look."

"You pox-ridden, cauldron-breathed fiend," I said and struggled to pull hard enough to keep the arrow from launching at me.

He winced at my insult and said quietly, "The difference between savior and sinner is oft merely who is left to tell the story." After turning away, he gathered his things and mounted his horse. "I have a feeling you are tough to kill, my huntsman friend, so I pray, whenst we meet again, you steer clear of me. Three strikes and I'll take you out."

I laughed because he really had no idea. Whatever memories I had to pay Morte to get out of this, I was holding on to *this* moment. And I would pay Mordred back.

Without Mordred's large frame blocking the light of the lantern, my shadow reappeared, this time oozing up from the ground around me.

"*Exactly how do you plan on doing that, you spineless, useless little twit?*"

"Hey!"

"*My time is valuable and I wasted it on you. Count on me to enjoy rending your soul to pieces. I'll make you pay for your capriciousness. I'll have an eternity after all.*"

"No, just until..." That's when my mistake hit me. I was going to say "just until Dorthea pulls me out," but to revive me, she needed to pour her magic into the opal. The one I wore on my chest—alone, in the middle of the Sherwood Forest.

If I died here, now, chances were I wouldn't be coming back.

"*Get on with it. The longer you make me wait, the more anger I'll take out on you. Each extra ounce of pain will be your own fault.*"

No, no, no, no, no. I'd gotten complacent, but there was a way out. I could just hold on to the rope. Someone would eventually come, and I'd tell them how to disarm the trap. Or when Dorthea realized I hadn't returned, she would come looking for me. Our bond would lead her straight to me.

"Rex!"

DumBeau stumbled through the trees, his tunic torn and

scuffed, but my abandoned pack in tow. With his arms out and a smile of pure joy on his face, he ran for me.

"Stop!" I yelled, but it didn't do any good. He kept running until he tripped over the rope, pulling it from my grasp. The arrow flew, hitting him in the shoulder and propelling him into my arms.

"Rex," he slurred. His smile growing bigger as he closed his eyes and went limp.

"No, hey, wake up."

"*Well, now, this is a surprise. Perhaps you are turning into a hero. After all, someone died for you.*"

"You don't get to talk, ash man. I've never wanted this."

"*Still, it is not enough. I'll see you in a moment, little failure.*"

I didn't even have time to figure out what he meant before a spiked log arced through the air on ropes, slamming into us like a battering ram.

We flew backward, landing in the lake. DumBeau was still out cold and weighing me down like a stone. I held my breath and tried to push him off, but my limbs weren't cooperating.

The water around us became tainted with tendrils of red. Blood seeped out of the arrow wound on DumBeau—and from a spike lodged in my side. I'd bet everything I'd ever stolen those log's spikes were tipped with cockatrice venom, because it was nearly impossible to move. So, thanks to Mordred, my story's end was a toss-up of whether the poison would reach my heart or if I would drown.

Pixing royals.

11

My Not-So-Fair Lady

Hex yes, I was bitter. I channeled that into anger, summoning a fury that would help me fight for my soul once I reached the underworld. Far more useful than hope ever would be.

Dorthea was probably wrapped up cozy with her prince, perfectly content and paying no mind to what was going on through our bond. But despite her self-involvedness, I was certain that if she were here, she would have tried to save me. Which was more than I could say for the revered Robin Hood—proof that some heroes really are zeroes with a good PR godmother.

That man never kept his word. He never showed up.

Why had I believed he could change?

No one changes.

My chest burned, and my throat spasmed, wanting air. *Looks like drowning wins the death honors today*, I thought as I sank to the bottom of the lake and darkness closed around me.

"*This is where love and trust lead*," Morte whispered.

A woman's voice rang across the water like a muted melody. "You said those words to me sagas ago, Nome King. You were wrong then and you are wrong now." I couldn't see her, but two dots, like pearls, shone through the murky depths.

"*Do not interfere.*" Morte's slippery voice took on an edge I had not heard before. "*Your time has long passed.*"

"My time is just beginning." With her words came a flash of light, which left me blinded. Heat seared and etched into my wrist. "I am the Lady of the Lake, and you are not welcome here. Be gone!"

The darkness receded and warmth surrounded me, like the water was wrapping me in a soft embrace. The stinging in my wrist cooled, but my lungs still burned from holding my breath.

I let the air out and sucked in a breath from reflex, expecting to choke.

I didn't.

"Dear little soldier," the sweet voice within the light said. "This story has not been kind to you. You did me a service once, so I have saved you. I offer you a choice: let it end here and dream peacefully in these waters for eternity. You will feel no more pain and none may harm you."

I still couldn't see the woman, could barely move, but I could breathe. Water. And I'm sure the Lady of the Lake was responsible for it. Her offer didn't sound half-bad actually. It wasn't exactly happily ever after, but it wasn't an unhappy ending or rotting in the underworld as a Forgotten either.

"No one would blame you for choosing the easy way."

That was a lie. A pretty one but a lie nonetheless. The faces of Verte, Morte, Dad, Kato, Dorthea, and everyone I'd ever met flashed in my mind. They all expected me to screw up, give up, shut up, and go down without a fight, so I'd be a gnome nut if I *chose* to prove them right.

Besides, sleeping forever sounded an awful lot like being dead. I still had way too much stubborn survival sense to meekly opt to count Bo Peep's sheep for eternity.

Even without knowing the second option, I shook my head.

Little bubbles that felt like laughter rose up around me. The warm glow intensified. "I knew I chose well. All of Story is flawed and broken. A dangerous evil is loose. Fight for me against the one who seeks to drain my waters. Be my champion, Rexi."

Amid the soft glow and lulling music and warm water, I needed even less time to consider the second choice.

"No way."

"Take up my—wait." The glow dimmed, the background melody stopped, and the water chilled. "What?!"

Breathing underwater was a foreign feeling, the water slipping in and out of my lungs. But talking was about the same—just bubblier. "No offense. But I did the servant thing. I was even a henchman for bit." I tried to shrug, but my right side, where the barb had hit, was as good as stone. "You seem great and stuff, but I'm done being a pawn. For anyone."

"But…but…" Her voice went higher in pitch, less siren's song and more siren's shriek. "I'm offering you the opportunity to be my champion. Don't you want to live as a hero?"

"No." I snorted, and the water went up my nose. "Why does everyone assume that? Do I look like the sort of megalomaniac who thinks they are solely responsible for saving the world?"

I was still figuring out how to save myself. If the world was depending on me, it was pixed. Of course, waiting for the likes of Dorthea to figure things out might be just as bad. But not my problem.

"Don't get smart with me, brat." Kelp shot out from the depths and wrapped around my wrist. It pulled me through the light, closer to the voice. "I gave you my mark, saved you from the Nome King."

At first, I was speechless. For one, her tone had changed very abruptly. But even more startling than that was the lady herself. I was used to ugly; I'd lived with moldy oldie Verte. But if the Littlest Mermaid had an ugly stepsister, she'd look like the belle of the ball next to this Loch Ness Lady.

Her skin was mostly see-through, understandable, since it

was made of bioluminescent jellyfish. The sickly gray fresh-water eels trying to squirm away from her head looked like hair. Her pearl eyes lacked pupils, which gave new meaning to "a blank stare."

It's a good thing I'm not as superficial as Dorthea. The most helpful people by far have been hideous, like Hydra. But just because the Lady of the Lake stopped me from drowning, that didn't mean I owed her anything. Plus, she mentioned I had served her once. I didn't remember ever meeting her, though I'd lived by this lake for years. I guess memories didn't mean much with Morte around.

"Whatever you did that lets me breathe is great and all, but you did that on your own because…" I may not remember, but I didn't want her to know that and think she didn't owe me since that was working in my favor. "…of that thing… that happened…that one time." I rushed through the lack of details and kept going. "The way I see it, if you wanted something more in return, you should have made the offer first." I rotated my left wrist to get free of the kelp, since the venom kept me from using my other hand.

The slugs that seemed to serve as the lady's lips turned up. Or tried to slime off her face. The effect made her seem amused. Her voice matched as she said, "You remind me a bit of myself, so I assumed you would not hesitate at my offer. I have obviously erred, yet what was done cannot be undone. Know this though: water is both life and death. All debts come due in the end. While it's true that now water cannot harm you, the poison in your veins will. Be my champion and help me protect the grail, or I won't stop the Nome King a second time."

"I didn't ask you to help the first time. This is my story, and no one writes what happens but me. And I pick the third option."

The Lady of the Lake let go with her kelp hand and scratched her head. "I don't recall offering a third choice."

"You didn't." With my hand free, I reached into my pocket and pulled out the glass-encased capsule I'd picked up off the shelf at the pawn shop.

Please work. Please work, I begged the universe and smashed the glass on the rocks under my back with a burst strength.

Just like before, when the capsule hit water, it split open, expanding out into a humanoid figure, this time without the princely head. As it propelled me up, I thought of DumBeau and felt a pang of guilt at leaving him behind. But thoughts were getting harder to hang on to. The poison must have finally worked its way through my system.

My eyes were starting to have trouble focusing, meaning unlucky death number seven was near.

Something disturbed the lake's surface. A hand, I think, dragged me up until air filled my lungs rather than water.

"Sprout. Sprout. Hang on."

Though my senses were fading, I could never forget this voice. Or the way he smelled like moss after rain.

I blinked and forced my eyes to focus the best they could.

Wanted

My lips were heavy and it hurt to smile, but I'd never been so happy in my life.

"Dad! You actually came."

I felt his hand squeezing mine.

Then nothing.

"Dear Stranger in Strange Land: When exploring a new place, it really is quite rude to roam around uninvited. Nowadays, most stories come standard equipped with some manner of talking-animal tour guide."

—*Dear Alice* manners column

Don't Fear the Reaper

Within a few grains of sand passing through the hourglass, my soul returned to the underworld office, the stack of paper on the desk higher than ever. I took great joy in swiping at it and sending the pages whirling around the room.

"Mother of Grimm! You get me for eternity, you son of a basilisk. You couldn't have given me one more curse-rotted minute?" I kicked the Forgotten-made chair, sending the left half flying into the wall in chunks. "It's not fair."

Wait.

As I looked around for something else to take my anger out on, I realized I was alone. The Nome King should have been waiting for me, waiting to edit me out of the story. I mean, this last death wasn't exactly a plot twist. He knew I was coming. Yet his office was empty. Either I had materialized in someone else's cubicle, or the boss was out.

"Well, since he's not here, he probably wouldn't mind me poking around his desk. And if he does, I'm already doomed to be a Forgotten. It's not like he can really make things that much worse."

I started ransacking the place, hoping to find my plotline. The office was mostly bare, but honestly, I'm not sure I wanted to know what the King of Death kept for personal effects. The knotted wire wasn't here, but without really thinking, I pocketed a bent quill tip that had been discarded. Dead or alive, old habits lingered.

The silver serpent slithered under the door, coming into the office. "Ssso much trouble."

I wiggled my soul's bare toes. "I am not above skinning you and making slippers. I've seen Dorthea make enough of them, it's probably rubbed off on me."

Instead of being intimidated, the serpent wound its way up one of the desk's legs. It seemed to chuckle, which sounded almost like crackling glass, and said, "You really have no idea. I ssssuppossse the Housssse of Emerald hasss alwaysss been full of foolsss."

Maybe if I ignored the snake, it would go away. After all, it was just a scalier version of the cricket nag, a manifestation of my inner thoughts of niggling conscious. It should be quiet.

I'd done a good job with this last chunk of life. I sent the frog back with a body and Hydra should be saved.

Hang on. I sorta kinda saved someone. Maybe while Morte was out, I should get a closer look at the compendium without his critical, creepy eyes.

His sickle and the book had been left out on his desk, like he'd rushed somewhere in a hurry. Taking a deep breath, I put the tip of the sickle to the page and scribbled my name: Rexi Hood. The ink skimmed the surface of the page…then dribbled off in a puddle.

"Argh! Son of a harpy."

The snake chuckled. "You were a loussssy henchman. But an even worse sssavior."

Pixed, I grabbed the snake just below the head and looked into its slitted, pewter eyes. Even in that position, she stared at me like she owned me.

"Griz," I said, twisting my mouth in disgust like the word was something her flying puppies pooped out.

"In the ssssoul."

I snorted and flicked her glittering silver scales. "Even your soul has tacky taste."

She rattled her tail, which would have been far more menacing if it had actually rattled. "My ssssissster will bring me back. You'll sssseee."

On the desk, the compendium rustled and creaked, like some unseen force was touching it. Pages flipped back and forth in a flurry until it seemed to settle on what it wanted.

One by one, several of the names scrawled on the page became unreadable, obscured by a swipe of white, gossamer ink.

James T. Hook
Grigori Rasputin
Pollyanna Crow

I would bet Mordred's name had been whited out on some other page.

"Yesss," Griz said, tapping her tail next to a name on the page. Grizelda De Ville.

We both waited for her soul to return topside, but the red letters spelling out her name stubbornly leeched through the white streak.

"Must be hard to reanimate a puddle," I quipped.

She shrieked, but without her stormbolts or acid-peeing puppies, she wasn't nearly as scary.

"Here," I said to Griz, tying her soul body into a knot around what was left of the creepy armrest. "Tell Morte I'm sorry I missed him. Let's not do lunch."

I couldn't record my name and I couldn't go back to Story for an eighth time, so waiting in the office for Morte to finish his Spell Checks or whatever was pretty much the worst thing I could do. But that meant going out…there.

Griz hissed and snapped as I stepped out the office door, but anything she said was lost to the howls of the Forgotten. Paper rained down from the sunless sky, some of it crumpled, some torn. Some with great slashes and symbols in bold red ink. Pages of stories that went unfinished and untold. I'd heard about it while serving in the Emerald Palace from sermons about the Storymakers that controlled our fate. The clerics of Libraria admonished all to pray for the Makers to show you the way. Then they warned that those who didn't behave or follow their path would end up cut out of the story and left on the underworld floor.

Seeing the blizzard of words among the cries of the Forgotten, I was almost starting to believe that there was a power that wrote every line of Story.

With no sun or moon in the sky, the only light source in Nome Ore seemed to come from bright flares in the distance. Maybe they were portals to other places, to other lands. Maybe I could sneak through.

Carefully, I navigated my way around the piles of souls and crumbling structures of unwanted and discarded settings. Slinking my way around, I stayed out of sight of Morte's copy riders—an army of identical, featureless clones, their entire bodies wrapped in scrolls. Though I don't know how they saw without eyes, they rode around on little creatures with shovels for faces. Like little paper pushers, they shuttled the falling pages toward the light sources.

This was by far the longest I had stayed in the underworld. After my first death, my soul looked much like a pale watermark. Each time, the transformation had progressed. This seventh time, my hands were still faded gray, but diseased black spots had taken hold of my toes and dark-gray tendrils were curling up my legs.

"Gross." I tried to wipe off my calves, but they were slick, like they were covered in smeared ink. The black glistened in the glow of the light. Which turned out to be a great blaze of ivory flames coming from a hole in the ground. So much for a way out.

The copy riders scrambled into view from behind the mounds of Forgotten. They scurried like insects, pushing unfinished manuscript pages into pits to fuel the flames. Like a forge—only instead of melting steel, they were melting souls.

I covered my mouth to keep from screaming as I watched more featureless clones tossing characters into the trough to be dissolved into ink.

I'd backed up next to a pile of decaying Forgotten characters without realizing it. A hand shot out and grasped my arm.

"Help us."

I screamed. I couldn't help it. When I recognized the face as Fryer Tuck's, half his jolly face blackened and crumbling away, I screamed louder.

The Riders ambled toward me, surrounding me and grabbing at me. I slashed at them with the bent quill tip like it was a knife. For every slice I made in their scroll wrappings, sans serif scarabs crawled out. For once, I didn't care about the bugs and kept hacking away.

But there were too many of them. They swarmed me, covering every inch and drowning out my screams.

Once again, I felt the familiar sensation of my plotline wrapped around my throat. Then it tightened like I was being lifted. As the bugs fell from my face, the first thing I saw were the white pupils flaring in the black abyss Morte had for eyes as he said, "I had hoped you would prove useful for my ascension. What a disappointment. There is a deadline to meet. I don't have time to waste on a useless story such as yours." With a flick of his wrist, he lassoed the knotted wire around my neck, then flung and discarded my soul in the forge of faceless shadows.

There aren't words to describe the feeling of losing track of who you are. I couldn't stop the forge from claiming the knots in my plotline as, one by one, they blurred and melted away, the memories that shaped my story erasing to nothing along with me.

For what felt like an eternity, I lay there, sinking and disappearing. Screaming until my voice was just an echo of a memory.

"I hear you!"

Dorthea's voice rang clearly, cutting through the cacophony of souls. The white flames in the pit burst higher and turned green.

"No," Morte cried out. "I can't let you out intact." He reached into the fires with his bare hand and pulled out a blackened and dripping line. Hurriedly, he started cutting off pieces with his scythe. I felt each and every slice like he was hacking away at my insides.

"Rexi Hood, vassal of Emerald, bound by blood, ink, and the curse in my veins. I name you as my creation and my other half. I order you to get your snarky self back here RIGHT NOW!"

Air filled my lungs so quickly, I broke into a round of coughing that made my ribs ache. I had been yanked out of the underworld.

"Welcome back," Dorthea said softly next to me.

Sitting up to breathe easier, my palm hit something dry and prickly. It was grass, yellowed and dead, as if the very life had been sucked out of the ground.

Verte and Oz stood just outside the dead circle, which was about ten trolls across, where the rest of the grass in the clearing was still vibrant and plush. The Maker's workshop looked like it had been hit with a cyclone. The chicken house was just gone.

What happened?

The opal necklace pulsed softly on my chest. Aside from one tiny thread of emerald running through its center, the stone looked orange and red, like a regular fire opal.

I turned to the side to ask Dorthea what had happened, but she collapsed flat on the dead grass. Her pale skin and flaming hair weren't bright enough to compete with a lit match.

Her chest barely moved. Mentally, I tugged the end of the magical string that connected us. There wasn't anything at the other end.

"Dorthea!"

I reached out for her, but Oz yelled, "Don't touch her!"

He was too late.

The second I touched Dorthea, the opal and my vision exploded in green flames. I heard a voice, but it wasn't Morte's. It sounded like several people talking at once.

"*So hungry. Feed us. Join us.*"

The flames burrowed into me, which was different from before, when she'd used me like a battery. Drain can be recharged. But I was being consumed.

"Stop. Please," I begged Dorthea, whose face was blank—but her eyes were wide-open and solid green.

The voices answered for her, braiding in and out of each other in a chorus. "*More. We need to be more.*"

I could hear Verte and Oz arguing in the background, but the curse kept talking. And a voice that sounded like mine joined the thread. "*We must take it and become stronger. Power fixes all.*"

No. I am a child of the trees…

"*And we will burn.*"

I could feel more than see Oz and his bright flare of power come closer. "My sincerest apologies, ladies," he said and bashed our heads together.

Then, blessedly, there was nothing. Just the lightest pulse of red. Like a heartbeat. Getting dimmer.

"4 apples, 1/2 cup sugar, 1/3 cup flour, pinch of baking powder, a teaspoon of cinnamon and nutmeg. And 1 clove—to hide the poison."

—*Killer Kitchen Recipes*

Food for Thoughts

I woke up feeling like how I imagine those dancing princesses did after hours of twirling in those ugly knockoff slippers. "Ugh," I groaned, holding my head in a vain attempt to contain the throbbing. "Somebody kill me, please."

"Meh, been there, tried that. It's actually considerably more difficult than you might think." Verte thrust a glass of something lumpy and brown into my hand. "Here, drink this. It will help."

I turned my nose up at it and dumped it out on the floor. "Call someone to clean that up. I'm going back to bed. Wake me when the kitchen sends up a beverage that's not poisoned. And preferably burrberry flavored." I closed my eyes and rolled over, reaching for the blanket, but there wasn't one.

"Dear Grimm, please tell me I was never that obnoxiously spoiled," a girl said.

"Don't worry, Dot, you weren't. More like twice that bad. At least," Verte answered.

I growled and sat up. "Would you two…" The sentence trailed off when I saw the girl standing by my emerald sorceress. She looked an awful lot like the Princess of Emerald having a really bad hair day. Which was impossible, because *I* was the Emerald heir, and I was sitting right here. "Who are you?" My breathing picked up. "Guards." I couldn't catch my breath and my chest burned. "Mother…" I looked down and saw that I was wearing some hideous necklace. Like a fire opal in a super-tacky pewter mount. But fire opals weren't more than half green.

"Yup. I was afraid of this." Verte stood up and grabbed my arms. "I'll hold her down. You scoop the sap off the ground and shove it down her gullet if you gots to."

The imposter princess did as she was told but hesitated when Verte warned, "Careful. I think she's a biter."

"Pixing right I am," I said. "Don't lay a filthy finger on me, you common street rat. Do you know who I am?" Opening my mouth to speak was just the opportunity they were looking for. The lumpy, viscous liquid was sticky, sweet, and absolutely didn't want to go down my throat. But it was too gummy to spit back out.

Wanted

The girl put a hand over my mouth and pinched my nose, so I didn't have a choice but to swallow. "Shh, I'm sorry," she whispered. "I'm so sorry, Rexi. Please be okay."

"Rexi?" I muttered behind her hand so it sounded more like "Mrphy."

Who the spell was that?

Out, Out Glammed Spot

Until the sap gloop stuff made its way through me, I *was* Dorthea. At least in my mind. Losing myself one knot at a time had been a nightmare. But at least I didn't know what I'd forgotten. Remembering things I shouldn't know…

I'd gone to hell in the underworld. And hell had followed me home.

After Verte and Dorthea stepped outside Oz's workshop to give me space, I found some ink and used a brittle twig like a quill. Very carefully, I striped my left arm.

"Didn't get enough of ink stains?"

I didn't acknowledge Morte and instead blew to dry the seven lines of ink. One for each time I'd died. With the memory lapses, it was obvious I couldn't trust my mind any-more, but hopefully I could still trust my body to tell the truth. For good measure, I added my name. In case I ever had the misfortune to forget who I was again.

Morte chuckled darkly. *"Didn't I say you were born to be Forgotten? End this already and submit."*

"Never," I whispered more to myself than Morte.

Even now, I still had lingering fragments of Dorthea's memories. Of Mom, erm, Queen Em. And trying to play hide-and-seek with Verte. I also had a wicked craving for chocolate wands. Worse than that though, her feelings…

I didn't know you could be so lonely in a palace full of people.

"Didn't you?"

"Get out. Get out. Get out." I scrubbed at the ink marks swirling up my calves, trying in vain to wipe them clean.

"I will not. It's my workshop," Oz said after poofing up from being in the form of that green book bug thing. Staring down at my legs, he said, "Unless you weren't talking to me." He combed his fingers through his mustache, his glasses wiggling into place on his nose. "You know, it's oft been said that hearing voices is either a sign of brilliance or madness. Now talking back to them—"

"Mind your own business," I said and glared at Oz. After I had come back to my senses, Verte and Dorthea had the intelligence and survival instincts to stay clear of me. The Storymaker lacked both.

He ignored me and grabbed my wrist. "What's all this now? Very interesting mark."

My shadow growled.

"I'm keeping score. Now bugger off. Literally."

"Pfft. Not those chicken scratches. The iridescent inked flower on the inside of your wrist."

He held my hand and pointed...to nothing.

I snatched my wrist back. "You know what's *oft been said* about people seeing things?"

He smiled and tapped his glasses. "I'd imagine it's said that they have eyes." He turned and went over to the lone corner of his crumbling workshop and started yanking down books and flipping through them. "I know I've seen that mark somewhere. But I can't recall in which fairy tale. Hmm..."

"Now who's talking to himself," I muttered. But that brought me 'round to a thought niggling in the back of my mind. "Hey, about voices..."

"Was it *Rose Red*? No."

I tried again a little louder. "Uh, I had this question."

"I know. *Janghwa Hongryeon jeon.*" He again ignored me and started tracing his finger over a page and mumbling words in a foreign tongue.

"OZ!"

He startled and tossed the book over his shoulder. "You don't have to shout. I'm right here."

I suppressed an eye roll. "Question. Voices. In the flames." I wasn't sure even how I wanted to ask this.

I didn't have to.

"No, you didn't imagine them." Dorthea knocked on the workshop's crumbling stone column. "Can I come in?"

I shrugged but said nothing as she entered. Dorthea called the green flames to her hand and twirled them like a jester's ball. "It's the curse. I hear them constantly. And the legion gets bigger each time I drain life energy. It makes me stronger."

"Makes you a nutter," Verte corrected, stomping in from the clearing.

Dorthea squeezed her fist and extinguished the flames. "Yes, that too. But every voice brings power and knowledge with it. Which is why I know what that is." She pointed to the underworld ink staining my soul and legs. "Why didn't you tell me you were being stalked?"

"Speaking of nutters, how could I explain my shadow can move on its own and is trying to devour my soul?" My face heated. There was such a jumbled mess of emotions in my gut that I didn't even know which one caused the blush. I picked my favorite—anger. "And who the hex do you think you are to lecture me? Saving you is what got me into this mess, and the only reason you know about Morte is because you and your curse took a bite out of my soul."

Now it was Dorthea's turn to blush. "I didn't—"

"You never do." The thought that she, of all people, had sifted through my private thoughts. What had Dorthea seen? That worried and infuriated me. "Tell me, did I taste good?"

Her eyes shot open, and Dorthea's blush turned to a queasy gray. "No, I—"

"I haven't seen Kato and Hydra. You're looking a bit chunkier than normal. Did your curse overeat and get them too?"

Flames burst out of her body, arcing in a circle, scorching everything in its path—straight to me.

"ENOUGH!" Verte shouted. The flames snuffed out at her command. "You both may be dumb as talking doorknobs, but I would have bet my *Sorcerer's Illustrated* collection that you were better than this. I've waited more than two centuries for all the pieces to come together, and I will not let you"— she pointed a shiny red nail to me—"or you"—she used the other pointer finger for Dorthea—"or especially you"—she pointed both fingers at the Storymaker—"to muck it up. Now, march. Everybody, go outside."

And we all did, because you knew a storm was coming when Verte's wart started wiggling like a weather vane. So it was best to listen up. Or take shelter.

Half the ironwood trees that formed the wall surrounding the clearing had rotted and fallen into twisted piles of bark. The rest didn't look too far behind.

"*Timber, little hero. I will see you fall soon as well,*" Morte promised as the sun shone on me.

A pile of leaves lay on the crispy grass, a stark contrast of alive and dead. Not too far away, there was another pile. Of bags.

"Where are we going, and for that matter, where *are* Hydra

and Kato?" I looked at where the chicken-legged house had stood. That space remained empty. If she had swapped heads, there would be a new shack. "Did she…" I put a hand to my neck.

Oz followed my stare. "Oh, she's fine. Both, in fact, are still with us, if that's what you mean." His brow furrowed. "Well, not with us, as you can plainly see from space-time theory. But that's here nor there, as in they are not here but there."

"There is where?" I suddenly felt like I had been transported to Suessville.

"Cam—" Dorthea started before Verte cut her off.

"Camping. Dreadful idea and you know this spoiled brat"—she nudged her thumb at Dorthea—"no way she was going to stoop that low. So Kato broke it off and ran away with Hydra. That Gwenevere, she's always been into younger men."

"*Lies.*"

Duh, and not a particularly good one either. Whatever was going on, they didn't trust me to know about it. With those two gone, there was just the five of us, if I counted Morte.

I smiled weakly and counted the pile of bags. Enough belongings for one or two people at most. "So should I guess? *We* aren't going anywhere."

I was getting kicked out.

Verte tapped the wart on her crooked, green nose. "Plain as this beauty mark, we can't stay here no more. And if you ain't figured that you and Dot can't be near each other yet, you deserve what comes next. I made a deal with you. Your service is no longer required. We'll take care of everything from here."

No, I wasn't getting sent away. I was getting left behind.

"*Abandoned again.*"

Again? What the spell are you going on about now? I thought silently at Morte.

He chuckled, long and deep, a sound that made my bones shudder. "*Very interesting.*"

I stomped my bare heel to get my shadow to hush.

I felt Dorthea's concern through our bond before I saw it on her face.

"It's him again, isn't it?"

I shrugged. "Not your problem anymore. I'll be glad to have this place to myself. Rots that you had to trash it before you left, but it suits me."

"It *is* my problem, and I'm going to try and fix it." Dorthea pulled a small notebook out of her back pocket and started writing. The ink was red.

As she wrote, the leaf pile stirred—even though there wasn't a lick of a breeze.

"Hey. No." I backed up a step. "Whatever you're doing, stop."

I waited for the green haze and power drain to kick in while the leaves swirled around my feet.

Stones rumbled behind me at Oz's workshop.

"Focus. Make every word count toward what you want." Oz poofed himself into a catterfly and hovered over Dorthea.

Dorthea scrunched her face and wrote faster, the leaves speeding with the fury of her writing. They plastered themselves to my feet, the stems digging into my shins.

I screamed and collapsed to the ground. My skin felt like it was being sewed with acid. And then, when the flurry of leaves was over, I looked down, horrified. "What have you done?"

"There comes a time in every marionette's life when you've got to cut the cords, you know?"

—Geppetto, *Planned Puppethood*

No Strings Attached

Dorthea leaned in to Verte, breathing hard. "Trying to protect you."

"With shoes?!"

The leaves had knit together to form a pair of knee-high riding boots. With heels, no less. Because that's totally what every girl needs for hiking through the forest.

Dorthea seemed to still have trouble catching her breath, so Verte answered. "Shoes worked before. If it ain't broke, don't fix it."

Oz the catterfly poofed into a rhimouserous, inspected his apprentice's work, then poofed back into a crotchety geezer. "Should stop the pestilence from spreading and keep you anchored in Libraria, away from the underworld and its price." He waited a beat before adding, "Assuming she did the spell right. I look forward to checking up in a week or so to see if the magic actually worked or not. Should be fairly easy—you'll either still be you…or you won't be anything."

What? Before I could question it, he swapped forms again and scampered off, ducking down into a hole. His workshop rattled and shook before squishing together, folding in, and getting small enough to be sucked down the hole after its master.

And then there were four.

After making sure Dorthea could stand, Verte loaded their bags onto a freshly carved ironwood broomstick. She returned to me with a leather drinking skin. "Those leaves came from the same tree as this sap. It's the last I could siphon from your tree. Drink some every day to keep the Emerald curse from nibbling at ya and to block Dorthea's story from filling in the holes." Her belt clouded over and her voice changed. "Be yourself. Ink is thicker than blood. Aim true." She thrust the bag of sap in my hand, wiggled her nose, then patted my head, like a good Dalmatian. "Hope you don't screw up."

After six years with Verte, I knew that was the best goodbye I could expect.

Dorthea wobbled over. I waited for a weepy hug from the future hero of all of Story. Instead she held out her hand.

"Seriously? A handshake?"

"No. I gave you a gift. You owe me one too."

That's the princess I'd grown to know and occasionally loathe.

I held out my hands. "Sorry, aside from this goop, I lost everything."

"Your necklace."

I was about to tell off her greedy butt, when I saw a vision through our bond. Dorthea sobbing into the opal, wrapping her hair around it to bring me back to life. I saw it through her eyes. Her memory.

"It's my fault you're wearing that horrid thing in the first place." She held out her hand again. "You should never have been tangled up in my story. Go find your own happy ending. I'll keep the light on for you while you try."

I nodded since I didn't trust my voice and tossed her the opal, careful not to touch her. Just in case the Emerald curse wanted to take me over again.

She reverently placed the necklace over her head and tucked the opal under the neckline of her tattered dress. Nothing else was said while she and Verte hopped on their broomstick. It rose, sputtering and coughing glittery smoke, finally lifting high enough to skim over the trees.

And just like that, they were gone.

And that left two, just me and my shadow.

Not that I cared. Just last night I was spellbent on leaving them anyway. So what if this time I was the one left behind? I stared down, looking for my shadow. "Guess it's just us."

Silence.

"Copy rider got your tongue?"

The echo of my voice was the only sound. With the second sun low in the sky, my shadow should have stretched long behind me, but not a black speck spread out from those enchanted shoes. There was nothing.

Not two, then.

For the first time in what seemed like forever, I was truly alone.

My eyes started to burn. I rubbed them with my palms. "I'm just relieved," I told the air. "Finally got exactly what I wanted." The barren spot on my chest, where the opal once sat, ached.

I slumped to the ground, like a puppet whose strings had finally been cut.

I had waited so long to be free. To have no one ordering me about, telling me who I should be, that I wasn't good enough, or bad enough, in certain cases. But I don't think I'd ever sat down and thought about what it really meant to be on my own.

So I spent all night thinking. Which is an absolutely horrible habit to get into. You can come to terrible conclusions that way. In fact, after a very long and silent night, I had one of those sorts of revelations.

Turns out, freedom felt a lot like being lost.

Everyone else had such a clear purpose. Even Verte had one…it just wasn't clear to anyone else.

Kato wanted to make his people proud, to continue being a guardian and return Blanc to her prison. Wherever he was, I'm sure he was still working with Bob, his overgrown, mangy butler who acted an awful lot like a dad. I remembered growing up with my dad in the Sherwood Forest pretty well. Trying to be one of the guys. To make him proud.

That hadn't turned out so well. I'd run away to try and prove myself and hadn't seen him since. But that was six years ago.

As for Dorthea, she'd become Oz's apprentice, so she could control the Emerald curse and get her parents back from the mysterious realm of Kansas. From our blasted bond, I knew that she felt she owed a great deal to her mother. I don't remember having a mother. I'm assuming I had one, since I hadn't hatched like a swan princess. When I tried to think of a mother, the closest thing I could come up with was Verte.

She clearly didn't want my help.

So as the first sun, Ethos, rose in the sky, all my thinking had led me to one conclusion: I was pixed. The only thing I had were my clothes, a headache from overthinking, and a rumbly tummy that sounded like it belonged to a bear.

Getting up, I stretched out my muscles, opened the drinking horn Verte had given me, and took a deep whiff. Then promptly gagged.

I'd rather starve.

I looked around the clearing. It was all brown and drained of life. Empty.

"If only Hydra were here, she could put her oracle head on. Then I might know what to do." I sighed. In the middle of the wish-pocalypse, after I summoned Griz to the Mimicman's ivory tower, her flying puppies had carted me off until I wiggled free, landing at Hydra's beach shack. At the time, I didn't know what I was supposed to do with myself—aside from stay alive.

Hydra asked me where I was headed. And when I didn't have an answer, she took me in and gave me this advice: "If ya 'ant to know where yous goin', you gots to know where yous been." Well, as I looked back at the roads I'd been down, there were wrong turns, giant sinkholes, and crevices where the path was just plain missing.

How could I possibly know what to do with myself when I didn't even remember all of my own history?

"History..." I said slowly. "Nottingham's Museum of Magical History." That's where all of Fairy Tales's magical artifacts were stowed away. Surely there had to be something there to give me a hand in getting a happy ending. Or at least a not entirely sucky one.

"Okay. What do you think?" I asked the air. Thus far, magic and I had not been a good mixture. "Yo, Storyfaker, you around? If this is a bad idea, send me a sign."

Nothing.

"All right, if this goes wonderlandy, I blame you." My stomach growled again. "Now, first step on the road to a fresh start should always be...food. And I know a hexcellent little bakery on the way, just outside the forest."

Head held high, I aimed to walk proud and start my new

life of freedom. I made it all of five steps. Heels were not made for hiking. They sunk into the ground, knocking off my center of gravity, pitching me forward to face-plant in the dirt.

"That's not a sign. That doesn't mean anything." Determined, I got up and, slowly, strolled out of the clearing, heading toward Nottingham. "This is way harder than Dorky made it look." And madder than a hatter with a mouse in a teapot, I made small talk with myself the whole way. Because hearing my own voice was far less creepy than the uncanny absence of sound that stretched over the forest.

Nothing tweeted or peeped. In fact, not a single animal seemed to remain in the dying forest. The ironwood trees no longer moved either. Perhaps their last bits of wild magic had left with Dorthea. But instead of returning them to the proud giants they once were, they seemed more like empty corpses. Like the petrified Forgotten.

"Ugh. Not my problem anymore." I needed to stop thinking. I'd already established it was a dangerous habit that didn't lead anywhere good. "I know." I cleared my throat and started to sing. "Let it go. Let it goooo."

"Yes, for the love of Grimm and all our ears, let it go."

I looked down to where the voice and accompanying snickers came from, but I still didn't have a shadow. The boots seemed to be doing their job, keeping Morte away. Except perhaps Dorthea had added a little something extra to enhance them. I hadn't been walking long enough to have made it out of the forest, yet I had covered far more distance than seemed possible. Especially considering my balance on the hexed heels was about as good as a deer on a frozen pond.

A line of guarding gnomes formed a barrier between me and Nottingham Pawn.

"Hey, pal," one with a blue, pointy cap said, hopping over to me. "Move it along. There's nothing to see here."

Oh, but there was. Something had happened to the shop. The thatched roof of the front porch lay on the ground like a doormat. The support beam was busted and splintered. Hex, the front wall had a person-size hole in it. Bigger than me… and I sorta had a vague feeling I had a significant hand in it being there. Though I didn't remember it happening.

Not to mention every tree, crossroad post, and building had a collection of wanted posters on them—Dorthea's, Verte's, Kato's, and mine, to be exact. Dorthea's and Verte's were dead ringers. Kato's had a drawing of a beast that looked like a lizard lion. And mine…well, I needed to send an apology card to my cousin, Red, when I had a chance.

Before the gnomes could ask any questions, I pulled my hood down and wobbled past them into the rest of the village. I didn't need a good memory to know where I was going, just a good nose. One sniff and I wondered if all the birds from the forest had ended up in the baker's four and twenty blackbird pies. My stomach rumbled, as if saying, *Who cares?*

The pies were waiting on the windowsill of the baker's

mill. The baker himself was outside fiddling with his water wheel. Every few seconds, he'd peer over to his window, his lips moving in a silent count. With a satisfied nod, he'd go back to his tinkering.

I still had the pewter button I'd nicked in my pocket. There was a metal bell just to the baker's left. If I could hit it…

I took aim and flicked it with all my might. The button soared spectacularly—in the wrong direction. It hit the blue, pointy gnome hat with a loud shatter that made me wince.

"Bogies, bogies. I'm hit. Gnome down. I repeat, we have a gnome down," the little guy hollered and hopped around before the cracks reached his mouth.

The other gnomes started angrily yelling, calling for vengeance, torches, and pitchforks. The villagers of Nottingham stepped out of their homes and their shops, staring openly and whispering to one another. They all gathered closer to the pawn shop. Including the baker.

Not what I intended. But it would work. A little bit of glue and the gnome would be fine. Ish.

With everyone's attention elsewhere, I hurriedly stuffed a full pie in my mouth and grabbed an extra for dinner later. Then I walked away, leaving town and heading the back way toward the museum.

A crack of lightning broke through the sky. The sound reverberated through my chest, down into my shaking legs.

"No…she's dead. Griz is dead."

But it wasn't the storm witch who soared through the sky.

A giant black-and-purple dragon circled overhead before settling itself around the tallest spire of Nottingham castle.

Malevolent had returned to the world of Story. And with another crack, she called down lightning and shattered the sign that had stood in front of the castle for ages. Nottingham's Museum of Magical History was no more. In a puff of white mist, a new sign appeared.

Academy of Villains: Fairy-Tale Campus.

Well, there goes the neighborhood.

"If you want to win big, you've got to scheme big. Have you ever heard of an evil overlord content to rule the trivillage area? No."

—Seven Habits of Highly Evil People

Hook, Line, and Sinker

I stared at the newly formed Academy of Villains and cursed at Oz, who, I had no doubt, was laughing somewhere. "You pixing rat, you know this is not what I meant when I asked for a *sign*."

My heart ached. Where were the Storymakers when I needed them? I had prayed all these years, faithfully hung Muse Day stars.

I shook my head and blinked away a slight haze of green from my vision. Me, myself, and I, Rexi Hood, had never once hung a twink-blasted Muse Day star like those suckers in the Emerald kingdom. Dorthea's memories had taken over, more wily and sinister than any villain in that castle.

Without thinking too hard about it, I screwed off the cap of the drinking skein and gulped down a heaping dose of my daily sap medicine. *Blech.* As I shuddered at the taste, my sudden urge to pray to the Storymakers vanished. And Dorthea's memories with it.

I sighed in relief. "That's more like it."

"I couldn't agree more."

Very, *very* slowly I turned to see who had spoken. *The* Evil Queen stood right beside me.

Without so much as a good once-over, she snapped her fingers and strode toward the castle. "It's been a while. Only fitting that you be my first minion in the new age."

"Me?" I coughed, my throat still slick with goop.

She stopped in her tracks and turned, rolling an apple back and forth over her knuckles. "Do you see anyone else, Huntsman? I'd hoped you'd gotten a bit brighter since our Snow White days." She narrowed her eyes and looked down at my heeled boots. "No, not my Huntsman. His daughter perhaps. Well, no matter. You are what I have. Not remotely fair of face, so I have nothing to worry about. Now chop, chop. The empress wants all the artifacts cataloged and secured by the third sun."

My options were pretty slim. I needed to get inside. And you don't say no to the Evil Queen, unless you are in good with a half or so dozen dwarfs. Or you can run very fast. Currently, I wasn't in good with anyone, and running was not an option in these boots.

Suppressing a shudder, I followed. "Yes, my queen."

"Perfect. I've so missed hearing that." She smiled, blew on her apple, and offered it to me.

I declined, saying I'd just eaten.

"Suit yourself. Now, get to work." As I passed, she grabbed my sleeve. "And one last thing. When you find my mirror, be sure to bring it straight to me."

The mirror. You know, the one famously on the wall. The one that could tell you anything you wanted, way better than any oracle. I smiled. "Yes, Your Heinous. I'll be sure to look for the mirror right away."

"Well done. I like a minion that's a go-getter. So let's just keep this between us. The White Empress never needs to know."

I stopped walking when I made the connection. "Blanc? She's here?"

The queen's face stilled, her wicked smile quivering to stay put. The smile didn't reach her eyes. "No, she is away temporarily on another matter. Apparently the museum was broken into and certain artifacts were stolen on the same day our empress was liberated. Speaking of which, as you catalog, if you, say, happen to find that mirror was looted...I doubt she would question it." Her eyes were smiling, if you could count a wicked gleam as glee. "So unless you want your heart carved out, let's make sure that is exactly what happened and when you *don't* find it, take great care not to speak to it." With that she turned away, dismissing me.

Super. Blanc was bad enough to make the Evil Queen

shake. And I was walking into the villains' new headquarters to steal from both of them. Swell idea, Rexi.

While the queen walked away, I took a deep breath. Slip in and get out. Just like any other heist. I'd find the mirror and be gone before Blanc ever showed. She'd probably blame the apple-obsessed royal anyway.

With a flick of the Evil Queen's wrist, the heavy double doors to the castle splintered into a thousand pieces. In the entry, there was a plaque: "Let this sword stand for truth and goodness, repelling all evil. Whosoever pulleth this sword from this stone is the rightful heir and king of all Story. Long live the return of the king."

Behind the plaque was neither stone nor sword. Looting indeed. Whoever pulled that robbery was a pro. But I had no interest in kingdoms or swords. While the queen retreated to the tower, I wandered the former museum's halls. Either looters or Dorthea's wish had trashed the place, hard to know which. Things were either missing or …off. The glass slipper was gone, but the fairy godmother's wand was still in its case. Sort of. It looked like it was made of chocolate. There was no genie, but then again, Aladdin's lamp looked like it belonged in a carriage shop, since it was full of oil. William Tell's leather huntsman bow had changed into a gold crossbow. It was tempting to make that last one go missing since, according to legend, it never missed its mark…but that's not what I was here for. I sped through the hall of heroes and went straight for the evil artifacts.

As soon as I entered the villains' wing, I could see why the Evil Queen had sent me. The black cauldron was a distinctive shade of puce, and its gooky contents were spilled all over the floor. Like a moat inside the castle. On the opposite end of the giant room was the mirror. It wasn't exactly an opulent wall hanging anymore. More of a handheld. Like one of those makeup compacts Dorthea toted around.

I looked around but didn't see anyone. "Hey, mirror." It didn't flash or respond. I called to it a little louder. This time a small comedy mask appeared in the silvery surface. Its hollow eyes managed to look at me, nonplussed. It stuck out a tongue then the surface blanked again.

Of course the mirror had attitude.

"I'm gonna have to come get you, aren't I?"

The face didn't reappear, but a voice rang through the expanse. "Why oh why do I get the dumb ones each time?"

"Hey! And that doesn't even rhyme."

This time, a tragedy mask appeared with a single tear. "Thanks to that wish, I've got a bit of a glitch."

Great. I planned on trusting my future to a broken magic mirror.

"Whatever, let's do this." If the skulls floating in the acid moat were any indication, crossing the puce cauldron sludge had been tried and wasn't a viable option. But where there's a will, there's an escape route. Running back through the museum, I grabbed Tell's bow, some of Rapunzel's hair, and the lamp after emptying out the oil. And yes, for the record,

I tried rubbing it first. Bubkes. With a little effort, I rigged up a grappling system. Sort of.

"You better still have perfect aim," I said to the crossbow. Targeting the mirror's stand, I shot the lamp I'd pierced with the modified crossbow bolt across the moat. The lamp-bolt hit the stand, knocking the compact into the lamp opening. The mirror murmured its unhappiness, but I didn't have time to care. The acid had already started melting the rope of Rapunzel's hair I'd tied to the bolt.

Hand over hand, I pulled the mirror to me, the acid residue on the hair burning my palms. Just as the tin bottom of the makeshift lamp boat started disintegrating, I yanked hard, flipping the compact in the air. I snatched it before it shattered on the ground.

"There," I said to the mirror. "I'm holding you now. Show me what I want, so I can have the happy ending, blah, blah."

With a misting effect, the smiley face mask appeared on the shiny surface. "If truth you want to see, then you need to be rhyme-y."

"Oh for the love of… Fine." I thought for a minute and spit out the first thing I could think of. "*Mirror, mirror, in my hand, show me what I need…most…in the land.*"

Seemingly satisfied, the compact tinkled, the reflection on its surface rippling like water before a scene came into view. Verte, Oz, and Dorthea were underground somewhere surrounded by chimeras. They were laughing and joking while Dorthea scribbled in her grimmoire, making Bob, the chimera butler's mane braid itself with bows and fire flowers. They seemed like they were having a great time. Without me.

I bopped the mirror. "You must be broken. Those guys are the last thing I need."

The scene vanished, the sad mask reappearing. "I hate this gig. Always the messenger's fault. It's rigged."

I put my nose up to the compact. "Look, you manic-depressive mirror, I'm gonna try one more time. That last answer was way too sappy. Show me what would really make me happy."

This time, a face appeared, and my breath froze in my chest. Kato. His eyes were full of emotion…full of…love. "No." I dropped the mirror like it was covered in the cauldron's acid. Letting go of the mirror didn't stop the flood of emotions and memories. But they weren't mine. The feeling of his wing around me. I mean around Dorthea. The feeling of his breath mingled with mine. No. *Hers.*

With fumbling fingers, I ripped off the top the leather pouch around my neck and gulped down the sap, not caring about the taste.

"This far from Neverland and I still can't help but run into you lost boys." Something metal scraped across the floor. "I'll be taking that."

Lost? He had no idea. I'd been too clouded by Dorthea's memories to notice the approaching pirate with a hook for a hand. I put my palms up. "I don't want a fight. Take the rotted thing. It lies anyway."

The pirate twirled his black goatee with his hook and cradled the mirror in his hand. "Mirror now small as a clock, show me how to beat the croc."

The mirror remained silent.

"Maybe it broke when I dropped it." I took a step back to stay clear of the villain. But the acid moat stopped me from fleeing.

"Or maybe the mirror bonds to whoever talks to it until the person's death."

"That's…uh…*parlay*?"

"Wrong pirate and we aren't in the Caribbean. Nothing personal," he said with a smirk before pulling me close.

"Unhand my daughter."

Even though it had been years, I knew that voice. It had a musical quality, a rise and fall that charmed my ears. The deep tones made me think of his rakish smile and warmed my spirit like the autumn sun. But before I could catch a glimpse of my father, Captain Hook's smirk twisted.

"As you will. No hands." Then without a further word, his namesake appendage ripped through my chest.

Hex on Heels

One minute, I was being gutted like a codfish; the next, I felt the sprinkle of something cold on my face. As soon as life flooded back into my body, I sucked in a huge breath and a little bit of dirt.

"Blech." Cough, cough. "Stop. Not dead. Well, not anymore." I brushed the dirt out of my eyes and looked up.

Robin Hood stared down at me. His beard was scragglier, with far more gray than the last time I'd seen him six years ago. But his eyes were still the color of spring moss, putting Dorthea's best emeralds to shame. And those eyes were very, very wide. Mouth too.

"Dad!" I cried and, in one motion, jumped out of the

shallow grave and threw my arms around him, knocking us both to the ground.

For a few beats, he didn't move. Then he squeezed me and pushed me back just far enough to examine my face.

"It is true." He squeezed my cheeks, turning my head from one side to the other, looking at me from all angles. "You're alive. And…happy to see me." He said the last bit slowly, his tone rising at the end like a question.

"Of course. Why wouldn't I be?" I hugged him again. "After I ran away, I didn't think I'd ever see you again."

"You ran away." Again with the raised eyebrows and tone.

"Hex sake, Dad, haven't you wondered where I've been the last six years? I wanted to show you I could be just as good as Will, Tuck, and the rest of the guys, so I snuck off and broke into the Emerald Palace." I tried to remember how I got trapped there and shoved in the kitchens and why I never tried to escape and get back to my dad, but there was a giant, gaping hole in that part of my memory. "I guess I wasn't as good a thief as I thought. You must have been worried sick. I'm sorry." The words came out halted and felt like spitting out rusted nails.

The blank look on his face morphed into the handsome smile that was famous for making maids swoon. "Water under the bridge, my merry girl. I was just beside myself for ages, but I'm a firm believer that we each have our own path to follow. It's very important to forgive. Let's not mention it again." He patted my cheek, then sat us both up. "I'm just amazed you're okay. I'd about given up hope. It's been three days since that fiend...you know..." He made a slicing motion, curving his hand like a hook.

"Three days? I wonder why it took so long to resurrect this time. Maybe because I'm so far away from Princess Dorthea and the opal."

Dad perked up. "Resurrect? Princess? Opal? I think you best be starting at the beginning."

"It's a loooong tale. Somebody could write a whole book about it."

"I'm not going anywhere, so take your time."

So I told him. Everything. The good and the bad. Well, at least all the bits I could remember. Because after all, if you can't trust your family, who can you trust? Blood is thicker than water, or something.

Dad paced back and forth in front of a giant dead tree. "So let me get this straight. This richy-rich brat made a wish that broke all the ties to our original stories and rewrote the rules of magic. And then you got suckered into doing her dirty work to fix it. For free."

"Well, sort of..."

"And in the process, you had your life essence stolen by the Storm Witch and shoved into an opal necklace, which you also didn't get to keep." He stood still with his hands on his hips, jaw ticking and lips pursed.

I squirmed under his glare. "You see, like I said, it's complicated. There's—"

"Ah, yes, I know. You got stabbed in the back by your friend."

I stood up, meeting him eye to…well, chin because he was still a lot taller than me. "Not by. *For.* I *saved* her. I did a good thing," I said, pounding my chest.

Dad put his hands on my shoulders. "And what did you get for it? Did this princess give you a kingdom?"

"Well, no."

"Maybe some riches?"

"No, cuz, you see, I sorta needed to redeem—"

Dad's grip tightened. "Says who? You did the right thing, and that book doesn't even count it. No, for your bravery and loyalty and trouble, you have the Grimm Reaper after you, then resurrection, death, resurrection, repeat. And all your so-called friends abandoned you without offering any help to save your temporarily immortal soul."

I stepped back and pointed to my boots. "Dorthea said she's working on it, but that's why she used her Storymaker magic to make these boots to keep Morte away."

Dad's face clouded even more. "What have I always taught you about these so-called muckety-mucks? If you want something—"

"You've got to take it for yourself," I finished and droned on, "ain't nobody looking out for you 'cept you."

"That's my girl," Dad said, ruffling my hair. Then he squatted low. "Now let's take a look at these magic freak boots. Maybe we can sell 'em at the market." He poked, prodded, and tugged.

Before I could say anything, I was on my rear, and he was yanking with all his might.

"Owowowowowow!" It felt like he was trying to amputate my leg.

He let go. "It's stuck."

"Ya think? Leave them be. Right now they're the only things keeping Morte away from me. Plus they're not *freak*; they're *unique*. Fierce haute couture." I stuck my leg out and admired the foresty fashion.

Dad's eyes widened, and he bit his lip. "Those monsters, what have they done to you? My merry girl wouldn't be caught dead saying something like that."

A wave of shock hit me. Then shame as I looked into his disappointed face. Then horror that he was right. To make matters worse, I realized I knew what haute couture was. Without a second to lose, I scrambled at my throat for the bag of sap and upended the thing to my mouth.

Not even a drop.

I shook it, then gave it a good look to see what was clogged. I felt like hurling. The drinking skin was empty, a giant hole cut right through the center. About the right size for a hook.

"It's gone…." I grabbed my dad's shirt. "A tree. I need a tree."

Dad pried my fingers off. "Look around, kiddo. You're in a forest."

"No." I explained the sap medicine. "Verte said she took the leaves and the last of the sap from *my tree*. If I can figure out what she meant, then maybe I can find more."

Dad pointed to the withered giant ironwood at the end of the decrepit camp that used to be my home. "Remember the stories I used to tell you about the forest? How the trees grew up from the blood and iron of the Holy Grail War?"

I didn't answer but rushed over to inspect the tree.

"Supposedly, that is the first ironwood. Sprouted from King Arthur and the black prince's heart blood. Don't you remember this at all?" Dad's voice lowered, losing its melody. No longer the fading warmth of autumn, but the sad bleakness of winter, his voice was grim. "You'd climb that tree and beg me to tell you tales. I could hardly coax you from its limbs."

If I tried to climb the tree now, I was betting it'd snap in two. The trunk was blackened and gnarled. The limbs drooped to the ground like a willow, like an old man with stooped shoulders. I pried the bark loose, but the underneath was dry. No leaves, no sap. Nothing.

Dad came up behind me and put a hand on my back. "It started to die the day you left."

I pointed to the rest of the camp. "And the rest? Where are the boys?"

"We all searched for you for years." He shook his head. "They didn't make it back. Everything fell apart."

He didn't say it, but I could hear his unspoken *because of you*.

My insides felt like they were rotting.

I am a child of the trees…

And the trees were all dead.

I sank to the ground. "What am I going to do?" My fault. It was all my fault. I didn't need the magic mirror to tell me what my future was anymore. Soon I wouldn't even remember any of my past.

"I'm gonna help you make it right," my dad said. "You can't save the boys, but we can sever the bonds that keep stealing at your soul."

"How?" I kept blinking to keep the burning in my eyes from turning into tears.

"There's only one piece of magic pure enough to break any binding spell and purify any curse." Dad ran his thumb across my cheek. "You and me, merry girl, we're gonna pull a heist with a bigger score than ever before—we're gonna steal Excalibur."

"Rule #2: In every story, the hero has a mentor who will guide and impart great wisdom on their journey. These mentors are often magical, sometimes animal, but nearly always rather cranky."

—*Definitive Fairy-Tale Survival Guide, Volume 5: Heroes*

18

Camelost

There it was again—a glimmer of hope, a sprout of belief…right before a heel squishes it out.

"Hate to break it to you, Dad, but someone beat you to it. Excalibur's already been taken. You were at the museum. It's gone."

He stood up and walked toward the lake. "It's not gone. Lost. And lost can be found." After reaching into his pocket, he pulled out what looked an awful lot like the compact magic mirror. "With a little help."

I was about to school him on the manic-depressive mirror's quirks, but instead, Robin Hood robbed from the wicked to give to the lake—or more precisely, he robbed from me and tossed it in the lake.

That got me to my feet. "What are you doing? How are we supposed to find Excalibur now?"

"That second-rate trinket couldn't track something as powerful as the holy sword of many names. To do that, we need to ask the woman who bestowed the kingmaker in the first place."

The lake bubbled and gurgled from its center, where the mirror had plopped into the water. The ripples grew and lit up. Mist formed along the surface, and a gelatinous sea monster with green hair and pearl eyes rose from the lake.

My dad, Robin of Locks—who swore he'd never recognize a claim of sovereignty over him—lowered himself to one knee and bowed by the shore. "Oh, lovely Lady of the Lake—"

"Lovely?" I choked out, stunned, while Dad shot a scathing look at me.

"Thank you for accepting my humble offering."

"Robin Hood, you have thrown many things into this lake maneuvering for something better in return. Yet, to bring this girl to me again, you are either a fool or more cunning than I had given credit for."

"Again?" I asked. I probably should have kept my mouth shut, but the legends my dad had told me had never mentioned the Lady of the Lake was a swamp thing. I wasn't sure what she would do with the mirror. I really hoped she wouldn't ask it about her fairness, because she wouldn't like the answer.

"I see," she said. Her blank, pearl eyes seemed to bore into me. It was an uncomfortable stare to say the least, and my wrist started to burn in response. I clamped down on it and slowly, like a gauzy curtain being drawn back, I had a hazy memory of nearly drowning in this lake. I'd made it out… except I had died anyway.

Remembering any more was slipperier than trying to hold on to the lady's eel hands.

"I'm sorry, Robin." She sighed. "Throw in an iron ax and I can return it to you gold, but I cannot reverse what has been done or remake her more than what she is. However, my offer stands. I can keep her in sleep at the bottom of my waters, so that the pestilence does not grow."

"There's another way. Excalibur. The sword was forged to break oaths and binds."

Her pearl eyes flashed. "That is a dangerous idea. Excalibur was made to unite the world under a single banner, to protect those who had been abused and oppressed. It is the liberator."

Listening to them talk, maybe this sword *was* exactly what I needed. I really didn't know which was worse, having my soul swallowed up by Morte or slowly having all that was me replaced by Dorthea. It was like being hung and burned at the stake at the same time—it didn't really matter which one killed you. Either way, you suffered, and the best you could hope for was a merciful arrow to the heart. Only that wouldn't work for me since I couldn't stay dead.

I wasn't about to bow to the lady, but I did soften my tone

and put my hands in front of me to plead. "If the compendium refuses my name and I'm destined to be one of the Forgotten, then I'm going to do that as Rexi, not a puppet of the Emerald curse. Not a pawn for Morte."

The choppy lake stilled, like a storm calming. "What makes you think you can retrieve the sword while the wicked, gluttonous witch still searches for it?"

I didn't have an answer for that. I'd forgotten Blanc was looking for Excalibur as well. Guess to be empress, you need the sword of kings.

Dad jumped in when I stayed mute. "My lady, you had to have seen how the tree glowed when I laid her body next to it." His demeanor changed so slightly most would have missed it. But I knew this smile, this gleam in his eye. This was Robin Hood, the man who could con Tinker Bell into buying a lifetime supply of organic pixie dust. "You said you could feel its presence in Camelot. Take her, and she'll be drawn to it." He clapped an arm around my shoulder.

Which I promptly shrugged off. "Camelot? And don't you mean *take us*? This was your plan. I'm gonna need your help to pull it off."

The jelly mass jiggled, swaying back and forth. "Whether Excalibur was stolen or returned of its own accord, I don't know. Magic has a mind of its own. But Camelot was recently taken over, and it's now guarded by a powerful force field. The only way to bypass it is through the waters of Avalon. All waters of Story are interconnected and, for the most part, still under my control. If you remember, I gave you a gift so that no water may harm you. I could lead you to Avalon, but unless your father has managed to steal some gills, you will have to go alone."

"But not for long," Dad cut in. "Have a little faith, kiddo. I am the greatest thief that ever was. I will go over land and find a way in somehow. And in the meantime, you can keep this with you." He handed me the golden crossbow from the museum. "You are my daughter. I know you have what it takes, and now you'll have my double bull's-eye aim as well." He put his hands on either side of my face and kissed my forehead. "I swear, I will do whatever it takes to free you of your burden. This sword is the answer to all my troubles." His smile notched up. "Our troubles."

The water gurgled. "I said I *could* lead her, not that I *would*."

"But you will," Robin challenged. "Time is running out. That witch grows stronger, and Rexi is your best hope of keeping Excalibur out of her hands. I have faith in my merry girl. I know that, when the time comes, she'll do the right thing and save us all."

Ropes of kelp shot out of the lake, drawing me to the edge. "Poor child. You didn't want to be a hero or a champion, so I will not ask you to protect the sword for the good of the world, but swear you will seize the sword and turn it back over to my care, if only to save yourself."

Now that I could promise.

"I swear."

"Then, Robin, we have an accord." And without giving me a chance to say good-bye, the kelp yanked me into the lake.

From my place underwater, Dad's voice was muted, but he said, "Find the sword and I'll find you." Or it could have been *Mind the swordfish or they'd skewer me*. Like I said, words were a bit garbled.

My eyes took a minute to adjust to the murkiness of the lake. But when they did, it didn't look like we were in the lake at all. The water wasn't cloudy brown; it was deep blue and bright corals dotted the sandy floor.

I'd been holding my breath out of reflex, but I couldn't stall breathing forever. A big clown fish and a smaller one with a gimpy fin darted to and fro in front of my face, tickling my nose. Without much choice, I sneezed, scaring off the fish. I tried breathing the water, trusting the Lady of the Lake and my body's memory that this would work out.

In and out, like normal. Just wetter.

"How are we in the ocean?" I asked, little bubbles coming out of my mouth.

"I said as much before—all the waters in Story are inter-connected. And I have dominion over them and all that reside within."

The lady had not changed with the scenery. She was still as kelpy and swampy as ever. But I suppose it made sense. Since she had domain over all the waters, her body was made of elements of lake, ocean, sea, and pond.

She still had ahold of me with her seaweed hair. And we

were going fast enough that some of the aquatic creatures that made up her body kept getting left in our wake—or eaten by bigger fish within her.

We didn't have time to sightsee, but to the right, a glint of gold caught my eye.

I dug my heels into the sand to slow myself to look. Seemingly out of place with the ocean's natural landscape were giant, gold fish gates. As in, a huge metal barrier shaped like a fish complete with mermen patrolling in front on seahorses and carrying oversize copper forks. A shiny, white coral castle glittered behind the barrier.

"Is that—" One of the Lady of the Lake's jellyfish zapped me.

"Yes, that is Atlantis. No, we are not stopping. Come along. No time to waste."

Dad had filled my head with more legends and stories than I could remember. After all, it was important to know where the best treasures were fabled to be hidden. I remembered that Atlantis was home to Neptune and his trident—a trident that was supposed to be glammed near as powerful as Excalibur.

"Can't we just—"

Zap.

"No. That would be one of the realms of water I do not control and where we are not welcome. They are on full military alert, so stay away from—"

I darted away from her before she could finish. Why go looking for Excalibur when another solution was closer?

Neptune was a royal. And thanks to Dorthea's hostile take-over of my memory banks, I now had years' worth of diplomacy lessons and how to princess pout stored in my brain. If I just explained I was working on behalf of the Emerald throne, I'm sure he'd be happy to help her out. Meaning help me.

"Excuse me." I waved to the very handsome mermen and batted my eyelashes like I'd seen Dorthea do. "I'd like to have an audience with Neptune."

The one on the left pointed his fork at me. "Be gone, demons."

"You haven't even heard me out. And for your information, I've been stabbed, burned, impaled, crushed, poisoned, and hooked. Oversize tableware is not gonna scare me." Diplomacy lesson #31: name-dropping: "If you won't listen to me, I've got *the* lady…" I turned around to point to her sludginess, but there was no sign of her except a few fighting hermit crabs.

"That's weird…"

Zap!

An electric eel's charge is apparently much stronger than a jellyfish's sting. Being immune to harm from water apparently didn't include the hazards in it. As I blacked out, I added electrocution to the list of ways I'd died.

When I came to, the Lady of the Lake had some words for me. Or, more precisely, she'd *left* some words for me. She'd stuck a note to my forehead with a sea slug.

I tried to warn you. You've been dead for days, and I had things to tend to, so I left my assistant to show you to the right tide pool. Assuming you revive—which you had better, since we have a deal and I'm holding you to it—Camelot has come under a change of management, so my name will curry you no favor there. Go unseen and do not speak to anyone. Return to the water with the sword and you will be free.

LL

Sigh. I once again had no memory of my time in the underworld, which scared the undead life out of me. Whatever Morte was up to down there was more than I could handle. Let the people with powers like Oz, Dorthea, and Verte manage it. I needed to be more careful. I looked at my arm with its seven stripes. I needed to add two more.

The Lady of the Lake had deposited me on a bed of algae in an underwater cave. Bits of crystals and aquatic pieces lay around, making it look like a home of sorts. In the center was a giant flip-top desk, fashioned from an ogre-size oyster. In its center, instead of a pearl, there was a glass inkwell with silver filigree. Pretty fancy. Probably came from a shipwreck.

I dipped an urchin spine into the inkwell, but the ink was shimmery and see-through. Unusable. "Too bad it's busted," I murmured.

In a nearby tide pool, a squid darted past. I reached in to snag it, scaring it enough so that it left behind some ink to use. One line. Two lines. Which made nine. I sighed. "Good thing I'm not a cat."

"Rex."

"Huh?" My head shot up, trying to track who had called

me. Despite the situation I was in, I couldn't help but break into a huge grin when I spotted what had to be the Lady of the Lake's "assistant."

"DumBeau!"

"Rex," he said again and moved toward me. He made it a few steps before tripping on his overgrown ears.

Sure, he was just a "thing" according to property laws, but I was glad to see the lady had managed to repair the sweet, dumb oaf.

I helped him up and tied his ears in a bow behind him. "There you go. That should make getting around easier." I was rewarded with one of his megawatt smiles.

His happiness didn't last long. His grin turned to a grimace at the sound of an echo deeper in the cave. "Rex."

"Yeah, bud. We've been over this."

"Rex. Go," he said. I didn't have time to be surprised at his new vocabulary. He shoved me backward into a whirlpool. Breathing underwater isn't the same when the currents are beating the pix out of you. It's like being a hand-wash-only cape in a washing cauldron set on spin cycle.

After what felt like an eternity, the water spit me out like a geyser, shooting me up and splatting me on the shore. My crossbow burped up promptly after. After coughing out half the lake, I crawled a few paces through the sand, until my hand hit something decidedly not sand. A black leather boot.

"'Tis you!" a man's voice boomed.

Aw, hex. So much for slipping in unnoticed.

19

Dual Deception

id you hope that revenge was a dish best served wet?"
Before I could respond, an ax slid under my chin, not entirely gently, forcing me to stand and look Mordred in his ember eyes lest I lose my head.

A black knight called to Mordred. "Iron and ashes, did you catch a mermaid?"

I couldn't see the knight's face behind his helmet, but I didn't have to. He wasn't wearing gauntlets, so I could see one tan hand and one very pale hand. But even gloved, I would have known that voice anywhere.

Kato.

As soon as his name filled my thoughts, the scene in front

of me changed in a flash of green. Kato was still standing close to me but without his helmet or mountain of black armor. Plus, though we were still near the water, it wasn't the Lake of Avalon. We'd been transported somewhere else.

The look on his face, the emotion warming his chilly, blue eyes—it was exactly the vision I'd seen in the mirror. "*Show me what would really make me happy.*"

And then I wasn't just watching a scene—I was living it.

Kato strode forward and put a hand under my chin, turning my face to his. "Right now, we're all we've got." His eyes were soft with an unfathomable expression as he placed his hands on either side of my face. "And we're all we need."

Then, without warning, his lips were on mine. I didn't understand what was going on. I wanted to push him away, but my arms wouldn't obey. They circled him on their own. Kissing him was wrong. I knew it in my mind, but my heart wouldn't obey. It galloped wildly, like a mount taken off the reins for the first time. There was no resisting it. I wanted to let everything go and live in that one perfect grain of sand in the hourglass. Except in my deepest core, I knew it wasn't real.

At least it wasn't real to me.

Just like Morte had made me do a half dozen times, I was reliving a memory. Only this memory wasn't mine. And it was a thousand times worse than before when I'd just known fragments of Dorthea's life. I had no more sap to bring me back to myself. And even if I had, would I have wanted to? My fractured soul warred with itself, one part wanting to fight since I knew this love wasn't intended for me, while another part didn't care and wanted to stay frozen in this moment.

Addicted to a memory.

Kato's nail brushed across my throat—not a gentle caress, but a sharp slice.

"If you like the touch of my ax that much, I can give thee more."

I blinked, the voice not matching the face. The green-glossed memory faded, replaced by the present. Mordred still held his ax at my throat. A trickle of warmth slid down my neck. I didn't have to see it to know it was blood. The coppery scent filled the air. I kept quiet, worried that moving my jaw might encourage Mordred to separate my head from my neck.

Kato stepped forward, taking off his helmet and dropping it with a clang. His face was the same as in the memory, but his expression was anything but soft. "I was not aware that the dark prince liked taking his frustration out on girls."

Mordred pulled his ax back a hair, relieving the pressure. "Are you daft, Sir Kay?" With a furrowed brow, he looked me over, then shook his head. "The maids from your land must look something foul if you mistake Rex as anything but an interfering huntsman's whelp."

At my offended grunt, he flicked my short, wet mop of hair. "Or perhaps a drowned rat."

"Rex. A huntsman," Sir Kay said slowly, eyebrow quirked high. "Is that right?"

I'd spent most of my youth trying to be one of the boys. But suddenly, it disturbed me to be mistaken for one. Or more accurately, have Kato think of me as boyish. But before I could stammer out a retort, Mordred lowered his ax and grabbed me by the scruff of my neck.

"Don't let the fair face fool thee. He's gotten the drop on me twice now. Nay, three times. If a mere lass had managed that, I'd be tempted to kill her and any witnesses just to salvage my honor and the pride of Camelot."

"Of course you would." Kato wiped a hand down his face and groaned.

"'Twould be a kindness compared to what the queen would do if she found a maiden had wiled her way into Camelot." Mordred shuddered.

Kato's face paled to match his white arm. "Good thing for us all that *Rex* here is just a harmless, sneaky brat, *who clearly doesn't know what he's doing.*" He emphasized each word, almost growling out the end.

"I don't think you give him nearly enough credit. I've let him go twice, thinking he was not a part of the Grail Wars. I won't make the same mistake again." Mordred squeezed tighter, bringing his nose down to mine. "It is as plain as your face. I must be getting close, and that's why you're following me."

"Get over your over-broody self. I'm not following you." My neck hurt, and my cheeks still burned from the invading memory. Full of anger and embarrassment, my heart still racing, I stomped on the tip of my crossbow—just as

Mordred sidestepped over the top of it. The handle whacked straight up between his legs.

Bull's-eye. Guess it had great aim even without the bolts.

Mordred doubled over, letting me go.

"So." I grabbed the crossbow and put some distance between us before he recovered. "Does that make four times I've gotten the drop on you?"

Kato half coughed, half guffawed.

"What are you laughing at, Sir Kay? Grab him. He might have already found the grail," Mordred said, still grasping his…knighthood.

"With due respect," Kato said, clearing his throat, "if your grail exists and does all you say it does, I believe your huntsman friend would have used it by now instead of…" He waved in the direction of the cross-legged prince.

"Look, I don't have whatever this grail is you're obsessed with. Don't know what it is. Don't care. This is about payback," I said, backing away from both of them. "In the forest, you left me to rot in that poisoned trap. But if you let me be on my way now, I'm willing to call us even."

"Yes. I think that's an excellent idea. In fact, I think it's best if we were *all* on our way," Kato said. Nearby, there was a high-pitched wail. "Ah, son of a basilisk. It's too late. That thing found us. We're all scorched."

"What thing?" I looked around, ready to run in the opposite direction of whatever was headed our way. Except what was walking toward us but a pygmy dragon carved out of emerald with a chip knocked out of his back. The tension went out of my stance. "Oh, it's just you."

Mortimer, the House of Emerald's guard dragon, snapped its mouth shut, its siren wail cutting off abruptly. He sighed heavily. "That's a lovely greeting. 'Just you.' Best I could hope for, considering. At least you didn't whack me with an ax, like some people." He stared down Mordred. "You are all hereby confirmed as absent without leave and are ordered back to the institute to see the director." He shook his head and mumbled, "Not that you're going to listen to me. I warned her. Can't get an ounce of respect, I tell you."

"What are you talking about? Who's *her*? And how did you get this far from Em—oof." Before I could finish, Kato sprinted for me at full speed. He barreled into my stomach, knocking the wind out of me and forcing me to the ground.

"Don't give us away. What are you doing here?" he growled in my ear.

"What are *you* doing here? And why are you squishing me?"

"I asked you first. But hurry. Hit me."

"What?" I froze. Kato outweighed me on his own, and the armor easily doubled his weight. "Have you gone and got rabies?"

"Fight back or you're going to screw up. Again."

My heart pounded. If he wanted a fight, he was gonna get one.

"Get. Off. You weirdo." There was a spot on his shin where his armor plate separated. I shoved the heel of my boot in the space as hard as I could. While he yelped and grabbed at his leg,

I rolled away. "Now, seriously. What is—eeeee." Mordred's ax crashed down next to my head, taking off a pinch of my hair.

"Stay out of it!" Kato staggered over and yanked Mordred's ax out of the ground. "This is a matter of honor. But I'm going to borrow this."

"Aye, if that's what you want, but don't hold back. He's a scrappy one." Mordred backed away. "Appearances are deceiving."

"You have no idea," Kato said under his breath and charged at me again.

I took off running, but the ground was sloshy and my boots sunk, throwing off my balance and sending me sprawling in the mud. Within seconds, Kato was on top of me again.

"That's good," he said. "Keep acting like you're struggling."

"It's not…an act." I squirmed to get away, but he put more weight on my legs, so I couldn't repeat the same move.

"Listen. We don't have time before the orderlies get here." With a swift flip, he rolled so that I was on top. The new vantage point made it so I could see the line of knights in white armor headed our way.

"What are you doing, Kay?" Mordred called.

Kato groaned. "Sorry about this, but we're running out of time," he said and threw me off, harder than he had to, in my opinion.

"Out of time until what?" I whispered.

He waited until I regained my feet and then tossed me the crossbow. My only choice was to use it to block his fake parries with the ax. With each clash, we continued our out-of-breath conversation under the guise of sparring.

"They're going to take us to Gwenevere."

"Isn't that good?"

"No!"

"But isn't that Hydra?"

"Sorta. It's different now. I don't have time for an explanation, and you're not sticking around long enough to need one. Just get away from here as soon as they let you."

"And if I can't do that?"

"Argh. You are impossibly stubborn. Just watch yourself cuz I can't protect you."

"I didn't ask you to."

The row of white knights had already taken Mordred and were just steps away from us. Kato finished the spar with one last swing of his ax, knocking me off my feet.

"No hard feelings," Kato said.

"Then what was that for?" I grumbled.

"Huntsman don't wear heels."

I looked down, and sure enough, the bottom of my boots had been shorn off. I had little doubt that wherever Dorthea was, she was horrified at the fashion mutilation. Or maybe those were my feelings. It was getting harder to separate them anymore. And I didn't have time to try before a pair of orderlies grabbed my arms.

"Don't struggle on the way to the headmistress, assuming you wish to meet her in one piece."

It's Only a Model

I complied with the orderlies' request because I really did not want to go into the double-digit death count, but also because I was pixing confused. Going to see Hydra should have been positive, but both Kato and Mordred looked as if they were marching toward the hangman's noose. The orderlies led us over the hill toward a huge stone castle. A sign stood out front. It did not say Camelot.

Academy of Villains: Legends Campus

"Change of management, indeed," I said, swearing under my breath.

I expected that we'd go into the castle, but we were prodded past the entrance to a much smaller version of Camelot.

Chintzy construction. More like a shack covered with an elaborate facade to mimic a castle.

Well, that solved the mystery of what happened to Hydra's chicken house. Gwennie apparently lived in a model castle.

An orderly knocked on the door, then turned tail and ran, taking the rest of the white knights with him. Mordred shifted from foot to foot, probably wondering if he could follow suit. A panel in the door slid open, showing a wide-faced old man with an epic amount of facial hair. The long, white beard curled in tendrils, like he had a hairy octopus stuck to his chin rather than a beard.

"Please tell me that's not Hydra," I muttered under my breath, just loud enough for Kato to hear me.

"Merlin," he answered. "And don't speak unless you absolutely have to, since you sound like a girl."

"And why shouldn't I? Isn't Merlin the guy who sent the fair-e-mrph—" Kato put me in a headlock, a hand over my mouth, cutting me off.

"The great and magnificent Merlin has far better things to do than deal with…" The man squinted through his inch-thick glasses. "You boys again. And—ack. You're multiplying."

"Why did the alarm go off? Did any girls breach the defenses? Drown them. Throw them in the lake. Just keep the hussies away from me!" a shrill voice called from inside.

"Just the usual troublemakers. I'll handle it," boomed Merlin.

"What's taking so long?" she yelled. "Is Sparkles all right?"

I pried Kato's hand off me and snorted. "Sparkles?"

Mortimer, the emerald dragon, ignored me and put his claw to his head. "I'll find a way to soldier on somehow, though I've been gravely wounded," he yelled loudly so the woman inside could hear him.

Merlin added another circle of glass to his spectacles, presumably upping the magnification. While he gave me a once-over, he chewed on his lip, which made his octopus-beard look like it was doing a jig. "Get out of my sight while you can." When I didn't move fast enough, he opened the door a crack and tried pushing me away. From inside the mini-castle, a chorus of yowls answered him and "Sparkles" slipped by Merlin and dashed inside.

Merlin grabbed my wrist. With a screech, he released his grip just as fast. "Bloody magnificent. What have you gone and done now?" he moaned, cradling his fingers like I'd burned them. "As if things weren't complicated enough. Well, you can't very well leave now. After that much cat-erwauling and the tattling gemstone nuisance, Gwenevere will demand to see you, *boy*." The door pulled open all the way, opening the air to the full effect of the meowing alarms. "Walk quickly through the catacombs if you value your hearing."

The catacombs was actually a hallway of crystal cat trinkets. They were all different sizes and colors. One or two had clearly seen better days, having been glued back together. But all were alive and howling as Mortimer trotted Mordred, Kato, and I down the hall.

Hydra's house was an assault to my senses. Underneath the meowing and hissing, I could just make out the steady thrum of a Taylor Quick song: *I knew you were evil when you walked in.* The smell of moldy roses lingered in the air. My eyes had trouble adjusting to the astounding amount of purple waiting for us at the end of hall. Rug, walls, drapes, and....

"Oh my Grimm."

I could only stare dumbly at the woman behind the desk. A woman wearing a deep-purple, dragon-skin muumuu, which considering her massive girth, made her look a bit like the dragon Barney.

Her head tilted a bit off-kilter, the gloopy neck stump making it easy to recognize her as another incarnation of Hydra. But I had to be looking at Gwennie, or rather Gwenevere, of legend. But Hydra showed not a single clue that she knew who I was. She was either a far better actress than she had ever given me indication, or Kato was right and this head transformation had not gone as planned.

Hydra/Gwenevere's hair was done up in an intricate spiral that framed her face, a face that was smooth like porcelain and just as flawless. The rest of her left something to be desired. In my defense, the body I'd fetched was a woman, and with curves just like Verte had requested. It's not my fault that she didn't say exactly how big she wanted those curves. Or where. The gut was a perfectly logical choice, really. But I didn't need stolen memories of Dorthea's fashion sense to know the dress she was wearing was a crime.

Wanted

"So you three are the cause of all this ruckus. Sit," Gwenevere snapped and pointed to a row of chairs in front of a large, wooden desk that was cluttered with knickknacks. The desk and everything on it was dusty and musty and completely out of place in the very feminine, lilac, floral-wallpapered room. On the desk there was a wizarding war trophy from centuries ago that had Merlin's name inscribed on it.

I sat down slowly, waiting for some sign of recognition from Hydra. Kato was still giving me the eye. Like his big, winter-blue eyeballs were screaming, *Don't screw up.*

The emerald dragon clamored up onto the desk. "I was just doing my job patrolling, and they came out of nowhere and attacked me to break the barrier." He pointed his gem tail at Mordred. "It was that one. The really bad man was the ring-leader." He sniffed, putting his head in the air a bit.

"Aw, now, sweetums, what has mummy told you? There are no bad men, just men that make bad choices."

"I could have taken him, but everyone knows the dark prince doesn't play fair."

Gwennie quit rubbing noses with the dragon and stared down Mordred. "I've tried to keep the past in the past, so we can focus on your future. However, you don't seem to be making much progress, so perhaps we need to rethink how much future you have."

Mordred stared back. "I will not apologize."

Gwennie stood up and walked around the desk. I think she was trying to slink, but, well, she more sort of oozed

157

and hoisted herself up on the desk in front of the prince. "You can't apologize since you clearly don't know what you did wrong."

"I told thee when I came here that I care not for your treatment. I live only for the grail and restoring Camelot to what it should have been before Arthur's terrible reign. I regret your trinket got in my way, but I did what needest to be done. That is not wrong."

Gwennie leaned forward and placed a hand on Mordred, her voice like poisoned honey. "What's wrong is that you got caught." She sighed. "I know you and my first husband had your little battle. You lost. So I need you to ask yourself: How bad do you want to win this time? Clearly your inept attempts are a cry for help. You've got to commit one hundred and ten percent. The only one standing in your way is you." She turned to Kato and ran the back of her hand down his face while he tried to suppress a shudder. "And you, you poor, handsome lackey. I'm afraid you seem to be doomed to be a hopeless underling. Keep working at it, and remember that the best endings belong to the bold." She turned to me. "And you…" She paused and crinkled her nose, her voice less honey and more acid. "I don't know you. Who are you and why are you here?"

"Rex, the huntsman," Kato answered for me. "He's my annoying cousin, always following me around. I was just sending him back—"

"Shh." She pinched his lips together to cut off his rambling.

"Lesson number five, Sir Kay. Mind your own business and look out for yourself if you want to stay ahead." She softened her face and turned to Merlin. "It seems we have an intruder in our midst. It is imperative that this remains a secure facility." She twirled her finger in his beard.

"It is, my lady."

Still intertwining Merlin's beard, she yanked her hand down while her voice went up an octave, rattling the crystal kitties. "Then what is *this* person doing here?"

"Well…you see…"

"Not good enough. Anything but perfection is a failure. Next time we could have heroes busting in, putting all our progress in jeopardy as they hope to make a name for themselves. Or worse, we could have an invasion of maidens seeking to be cursed or take my rightful place." She let go of Merlin and inched closer to me. "In fact, maybe it's too late. You don't look manly enough to be *the* Huntsman."

Now I was starting to see why Kato had warned me off. I was also starting to worry that the Gwennie head had been in that ironwood lockbox for a very good reason.

"It's just like, um, Kay said. Except I'm not *the* Huntsman. Just his kid." I coughed. "His son. Nope, no girl cooties on me. Takes a man to live in the forest, my dad always said," I added, pitching my voice lower. The last part was true at least. "Anyway, I've heard about your school. And I'm here to learn. Stuff."

Kato sighed heavily and scrunched up his face. I rolled my

eyes. Maybe I'd said the wrong thing, but Gwennie stopped looking like she wanted to eat me.

"Yes, I think I've read a bit of your story. I can see the resemblance to your father. You certainly look weak and could benefit from our treatments. So if that's to be the case, let us seize the day and get started."

"Wait…treatments?"

She ignored me and picked up a spellphone. "It's me. Gather the patients…mmmhmm. Yes, we are having an impromptu group therapy session." She paused. "Oh…I'm thinking at the Globe, so ready the unicorns for the treatment."

A pair of orderlies grabbed my arms and marched me out before I could even say, "Unicorns?"

21

Extreme Group Therapy

The orderlies led us back down the hill and to a round barnlike building made of wood and stone. At the entrance, the guys were led to the left, while I got nudged right. I was not a princess, so I can only blame Dorthea's bond intruding again, but as we passed the stables, I couldn't help but squeal.

"They're so cute!" Each stall housed a miniature pony. Some were unicorns, some were pegasi, but all had vibrant and colorful coats, manes, and tails. They were abso-pixing-dorable. "Can I pet one?"

My guards snickered at me. "You'll get your chance."

They prodded me to keep walking. As I passed, a little,

pink pony sneezed, spraying glitter every which way. Maybe this unicorn-therapy thing wouldn't be so bad.

The first sign that I was wrong was quite literally more signs. Brightly colored art hung on the wooden support beams. Some were finger paintings, or tentacle paintings, I suppose, since they seemed to be signed by Cthulhu. Next, I passed a poster proclaiming "Hang in there," which pictured a man in black hanging from a noose in a tree. But he was giving a thumbs-up, so I guess the visual was supposed to be encouraging.

After a few more depressing motivational posters, I exited the round hall and walked into a dirt-floor arena. Merlin and Gwenevere waited alone in the middle, but I could hear rustling and stomping from all directions. I turned and looked around. Another sign that this was not going well? I had an audience.

Orderlies led Kato, Mordred, and who I assumed were the other "patients" into balconies painted in happy primary colors. It looked like a rainbow had thrown up in here. And at a glance, the audience looked like the who's who of wanted posters, except in this setting, they looked more pathetic than powerful. Aladdin's evil sorcerer petted a stuffed parrot on his shoulder. A skeevy pirate glared at me while twirling his bluebeard. Even the really pale guy with a cap and fangs didn't look too intimidating when he was plopped down on a sunny-yellow beanbag chair. Plus, his skin sparkled when the light hit him.

But it was the middle of the arena that made alarms go off

in my brain, louder than if the hunchback rang the bells in my belfry. Merlin took two steps to the side, revealing a post with built-in shackles.

I cursed and struggled while the orderlies chained me to the post. "I thought this was a school. What the hex?"

Gwennie smiled broadly and gave my cheek a pinch. She turned to the balconies of beanbags. "Hello, my dear men. Welcome to today's meeting of Villains Anonymous. Before we say our affirmations, I will let our newest initiate introduce himself."

I glared and clamped my mouth shut.

Gwennie tsked. "Admitting you have a problem is the hardest part, and we are all here to help you through the steps. Everyone say hello to Rex."

"Hello, Rex," dozens of voices unenthusiastically hollered back.

Gwen continued, "When Merlin asked me to head up this little academy, it was a horrible place to learn to be vile." The crowd grumbled. "Relish in the suffering of others." More murmurs, some excited. "Act downright cruel." That one got a bit of applause. "It broke my heart." Gwen put her hand to her chest. "Those behaviors will only give you temporary joy, not a lasting happy ever after. What you need is love."

There was no reaction from the audience.

While cheesy, Gwen's philosophy sounded okay. Maybe this would work out after all.

Gwennie's lip quivered, and she fanned invisible tears.

"You need to love yourselves and find pride in your villainy if you want to succeed in taking over the world. Which is why I took over and transformed this abysmal place into the Enlightened Villains Institute and Laboratory."

"Wait, what?" I said over the audience's standing ovation.

"Now, everyone, say the serenity prayer with me."

"There is serenity in my villainy," everyone said in unison. "Storymakers crafted me a story I could not change. But now I will find the courage to change what I can. And *take* the power to make up the difference."

Their booming voices hit my chest like a drum.

"What is this?" I asked Gwen while villains hugged it out and shook hands. "The rules of Story got busted, so now it's an evil free-for-all where good isn't guaranteed to win?"

"Perception is reality." With a snap, she had two orderlies bring over a king-size mirror and place it right in front of me, so I was forced to look at my reflection. "Take a good look. What do you see?"

It was the first chance I'd been able to get a good peek at myself for a while. My short, blond hair was drying from my swim in the lake and starting to poke up again. Lake muck was smudged over a good bit of my face. And the leather Huntsmen-line hooded coat I'd swiped from DumBeau back in the forest really *did* make my shoulders look broader. I looked anything but feminine.

Which was good, since it seemed that Gwenevere had a jealous streak wider than her waistline.

"A huntsman," I answered.

"These mirrors no longer show what is real. So we have to use a few other tricks." She blew some glitter at me. "Tell me again: What do you see?"

I saw the same reflection. But instead I replied, "A nobody."

Gwennie grinned widely. "Yes, that's what all those who write the stories want you to believe. That you are a nobody. That you're no good. A lowlife hood."

I chuckled because she might be speaking to Rex the Huntsman, but the same applied to Rexi Hood.

"I'm telling you that there is no evil or good. There is only success or failure. The winner gets called a hero and the loser, a villain or a Forgotten. Well, who says the good guy wins?" She turned to the crowd and smashed the mirror to the ground. "Who says *we* are not the good guys? We need to be honest about who and what we really are and stop being ashamed of ourselves. We need to stop sabotaging ourselves because we don't think we are worth it." Her tone quieted. "You, Rex, are worth it."

My eyes were warm and wet from the glitter. It had nothing to do with the fact that it was the first time anyone had ever said anything like that to me. What she said made more sense than anything I'd heard in ages.

"Now prove it." She yelled to the orderlies, "Release my little ponies! I'll be in my rooms. Send him to me if he survives the first trial."

Gwen hastily made an exit.

Survives? I shook my head to clear the glitter out of it. I'd forgotten I was tied to a stake.

Merlin had made his way to the edge of the arena too. He read from a clipboard with an abbreviation on the back: E. V. I. of L. "Let the trial of honesty and loyalty begin. You must be open to change. Lie to yourself and perish. Question number one: Why are you here?"

As the bright, poofy teacup unicorns trotted in, I figured this couldn't be too bad. "Are they gonna kill me with cuteness?" I snickered at the absurdity, then told Merlin what he wanted to hear. "I want to be a great villain."

The purple-haired unicorn closest to me turned black, its mane bursting into bright-blue flames.

Merlin twirled his beard. "These are the queen's special unicorn-night-mare hybrids. The unicorn half is drawn to goodness, purity, and maidens. While the night mares are angry beasts trained to flame out deceptions. I suggest you not lie or you will burn at the stake," he said, before mouthing so no one but me could hear, "Rexi."

"Honesty is absolutely the best policy. At least until I can afford a nose job."

—Pinocchio, Page Pix gossip column

The Naked Truth

Merlin knew my true identity? Maybe I'd heard him wrong. I was a bit distracted by the thought of being roasted alive.

I didn't have time to worry about it though, because Merlin had already jumped to question number two. "Do you believe you are the narrator of your own story?"

"Yes."

Another harmless-looking, pink flufflepuff went up in flames, sending sparks in my direction.

"Question number three: Do you think you deserve to be happy?"

"Of course. Who doesn't?"

The last five unicorns lit up like Jack's candlesticks. The crowd started cheering, or maybe that was the blood thrumming in my ears. Sweat beaded on my face as the teacup night mares and the wall of heat they produced got closer.

"Question number four: Are you willing to join our cause and take this world back from the heroes?"

"Can't I just sit this round out? I'm quite happy with the way I am. I changed my mind."

The mini-unicorn that used to be pink sneezed, but this time instead of spewing glitter, sparks flew, landing at the base of the stake. The wood smoked, then crackled and popped as flames sprouted. And spread.

Merlin fluffed his suit and sneered. "I'm really not surprised you're failing this trial so abysmally. Looks like your life hangs on question number five: What are you afraid of?"

"Bugs."

There were no new sparks, but the flames inched their way up the stake. The crowd chanted, "Burn, burn."

"Not good enough. Go deeper," Merlin prodded.

Oh, that was a trick question. I locked stares with Kato in the stands. He looked torn. He'd warned me he couldn't help me. I didn't want him to, but why couldn't he just leave? I didn't want him to see me die, or worse—to see the real me.

My story really was cruel.

I took in a deep breath and let it all go. "I'm afraid of disappearing. Of losing everything I am. Or that what I am isn't worth saving in the first place and that I'll be gone and no one will notice."

The nightmare flames snuffed out, cooling the wall of heat and turning the night mares back into the horribly evil cute ponies. But the post still crackled and flames licked past my boots and up my legs. Merlin walked toward me, pulling a glass of water out of his pointy hat. The smell of rosewater filled my nose.

"Tell me, girl," he whispered. "What are you willing to do to keep that from happening?"

"*Anything*," I wrenched out, straining against the chains.

"Good answer," he said and extinguished the flames. He turned to the audience. "Welcome our newest *brother*, Rex."

The fickle crowd went from cheering for my demise to running down to the arena floor, each taking a turn to greet me. Their welcoming was conveyed in universal guy code, with smacks on the arm by their fists...or tentacle, or whatever. I refused to look at Kato as he passed. And Mordred, well, let's just say he punched extra hard.

"There is something about thee I just really can't stand. No one else may see it, but thou art dangerous. Stay away from what is mine," he hissed.

"No problem, psycho," I muttered, worn-out.

After everyone had their turn, the orderlies pulled me off the stake and dragged me back to Gwenevere. I went amiably, because I was too exhausted to move. Whatever I had been expecting from this journey, this hadn't been it. I didn't know whether to cry, run screaming, look for an aloe plant, or find that stupid sword and get the hex out of Camelot.

The crystal kitties began their chorus.

I glared at them and hoped they had their ears open. "I swear to any of you that will listen, if you keep up that shrieking, I will pound each and every one of you into glitter to feed you to those blasted unicorns."

"I see you've found your fighting spirit," Gwennie chirped in a high-pitched, cheery voice that was almost as annoying as the cats. "You are a lot less charbroiled than I expected. Perhaps there's hope for you yet."

"Does everyone go through that?"

"No, just the poor, unfortunate souls I really don't like."

"Great," I huffed. "Now what? Since I passed, can I get the grand tour? See all the famous Camelot artifacts?" *Like a certain sword.*

"I'll need you to sign a few waivers. Then you can go get some rest. I've assigned you to a ward with a sponsor as your roommate." She laid down a piece of parchment. "Initial here, here, and…" She pointed out a few more spots, then flicked the paper till it rolled open like a scroll. "And sign your full name at the very bottom."

"Fine print much?" The more the scroll went on, the smaller the letters became, but I was pretty sure a number of clauses released the institute from liability in case of death, dismemberment, or transmogrification.

"All standard consent forms, I assure you. The demon

lawyers at Gold Man's Sacks are very trustworthy." Gwen peered into the drawers of the desk. "Now where did I put that pen?"

I skimmed the desktop while she scavenged. A lot of random stuff. Flask of cauldron juice. Stuffed owl. Beard trimmer. Granite paperweight. It had a pen in it.

"I can use that one," I said.

"It's broken and useless like everything else on this ridiculous wizard's desk." She resumed her search, crawling around on the floor.

I just wanted to be done. I removed the silver-and-sapphire pen and put it to the parchment.

A crack sounded from outside, and a strange light hit the heavy, purple curtains, casting the whole room in a violet haze. Gwennie bolted upright. "What was that?" She ran/waddled to the window to investigate.

As long as the lightning stayed out of my way, I didn't care what it was.

I went back to the paper and scribbled a bit. For a second, I flashed back to the *Compendium of Storybook Characters*. I half expected my name to be banned from any record. But the ink seemed to flow and write just fine, so I initialed *R. H.* and remembered to sign *Rex the Huntsman* at the bottom. "Done," I said, pocketing the broken pen.

Gwen shrugged and turned back to me. "Something broke the old sign. I'd been meaning to have it replaced with the institute's new placard anyway. Now, where were we?"

"Room. That place where, according to the contract you just had me sign, I can check in anytime I like, but I can't ever leave."

Gwen frowned and reached for my hand. "Do try to have a positive attitude. I run a very tight operation. But it really is with your safety in mind." She squeezed, digging her nails into me, drawing blood. "I will not allow anything or anyone to bring chaos to the order I've created. We don't tolerate failures. Are we clear?"

"Crystal," I said and yanked my hand back.

"Good," she replied and licked her nails. "Here's your room assignmen—" She paused, her head shaking, nose twitching, lips quivering. She sneezed. I half expected glitter or fire to come out of her, just like her beasts, but instead, her forehead lined with wrinkles, her perfect face no longer flawless.

She blinked. "Hot glammed, 'bout time." She blinked again, looking at me as if really seeing me for the first time. "Rexi? What are you doing here, you idgit? Yer gonna ruin everything."

"Hydra," I said slowly and carefully.

"The one and only...fer a minute. Or less. I knews you were trouble when you washed up on my beach, not once but twice! Now you Mary Poppins up right in front of me again. Git."

Maybe I trusted her, or maybe the truth worked. Either way I couldn't lie. "No can do. I can't go until I get Excalibur."

"Join the club. More ozmosis, I tell you. Only a magic sword would think of playing hide-and-seek, but I can tell it's here in Camelot. Somewhere close." She looked at the paper. "You would have been wolf kibble if I hadn't shown up." She pointed out my room assignment. Listed under sponsor was B. B. Wolfe. Hydra's nose twitched. "Ah, bugger me. She's coming back. My mama warned me that the first head was always the most trouble. But did I listen. No? I had to pick a doozy. Should have gotten a nice, dumb kitchen girl like you. But no, I wanted a royal." Sigh. "I never could rein her in." She scribbled a number on my hand. "Go here. Best I can do to keep your secret. Do *not* trust anyone but Kato. Even me…ah…ah…hurry…"

I ran out the door before she sneezed again.

Mortimer, a.k.a. Sparkles, waited for me at the door with the crossbow that the orderlies had taken from me earlier. "I know who you are, you know. You tried to steal me once."

Oh great. "Sorry. You can't tell anyone." I racked my brain for what I could give or threaten to make the little dragon keep its snout shut.

He pointed his tail up to the highest window, where Merlin twirled his curly beard. "Already covered. And besides, you used to polish my scales at the Emerald Palace. And even though you tried to steal me, you never tried to *break* me, which is more than I can say for some uncivilized brutes." He sniffed. "All this espionage is too much for me. I miss my perch and Verte."

"How did you get here?" I'd guessed he was in a million pieces in the crater that used to be the Emerald Palace.

"Gwenevere remade me to suit her needs. The Pendragons have a gift with crystal and gemstones." He sighed. "I do think she could have made me a bit bigger this time. It really would be the least they can do." He spoke quietly. "Merlin promised an upgrade if I…" He used his claw to mime locking his lips.

"Okay…" Even without Hydra's warning, trusting Merlin was not on my to-do list. There was something off about him, and somehow he knew who I was. He didn't seem keen on exposing me—yet. Which meant he wanted something.

"That is you." Mortimer pointed to a solid oak door in the interior of the castle, at the end of the corridor. "You are on your own," he said and scampered away.

"Weird little dragon." The path had cobwebs, like no one used it much. I didn't like bugs, but I disliked villainous roommates more, especially ones who had a history of violence toward the extended Hood family. Since Hydra was protecting my secret, I figured I'd have a single, unused room. It would be nice to have some privacy.

"Thank goodness Hydra showed up when she did," I muttered to myself and threw open the door. It oofed.

After stepping in, I slowly closed the door, hand on my crossbow, just in case.

As the door creaked shut, it revealed the source of the mysterious sound.

Heart Attacks

Kato growled, wearing a scowl—and not a whole lot else. I'd seen the show when Hydra witch doctored him from beast to boy. This was different. Back then, I thought of him like a stupid older brother. Now...suddenly I couldn't get my mind off the kiss lodged in my memory. The butterflies in my chest turned to frenzied bats, and I bolted from the room, slamming the door on the way out.

I thought I felt hot during the honesty trial. Those nightmares were subzero next to the heat in my face, and I was pretty sure I could add "die by embarrassment" to my list.

"Please let the melodramatic dragon be dyslexic."

I looked at the scrawl on my hand. 228. I looked at the door. No luck. 228. I was exactly where Hydra wanted me.

I paced back and forth in front of the door to get myself together and give Kato a chance to not be buff in the buff before I went in again. I was so pixed. This really couldn't get any worse.

"This isn't real. These aren't my feelings. They're fake, an illusion. I don't want him. Dorthea does." My pulse disagreed. So did the flood of memories that washed over me. I didn't want to know what it felt like to be in his arms. To be protected. Valued. Loved. I had never hated Dorthea more than I did in that one moment, for this unique bit of torture, for her memories of a life that I could never have—that I would never have wanted if I hadn't seen how wonderful it could be. It was so cruel to give me a taste of happiness that wasn't mine.

The world is yours if you take it.

Morte? No, the voice wasn't the slippery ink of the Grimm Reaper. It was the twisted chorus—the Emerald curse.

I closed my eyes, and for a moment, I could feel her, feel Dorthea, wherever she was. I was her; she was me. We were one. I leaned against the door and put out my hand.

That's it. Feed us more power.

If I tried…I could call the emerald flames to my hand, just like Dorthea. I knew it. Then I could just—

In a fraction of a second, I went from standing in the hall to laying flat on my back inside the room. A jarring whack to the head broke the curse's hold on me for the moment. I opened my eyes and looked up to thank Kato for opening the door at exactly the right moment.

The unamused eyes were not the ones I expected.

That whole "can't get any worse" thing? I had to stop thinking that, because it always came true.

"Hi, roomie," I said to Mordred, waving a hand in front of my face, less as a way of greeting, more so to have a chance to block a punch.

Mordred glanced back and forth between me and Kato, who was now dressed but taking deep breaths and tapping his black, broken fingernails on his chin. "What is it with the two of thee? Sir Kay, thou didn't seem to know this rascal, yet now you claim him as kin? And, Rex, what part of my warning did thee not understand? Stay. Away."

I couldn't help it; the guy just hexed me the wrong way.

"Aww, yeah, sorry. I only heard the stay part." I lifted my hand, showing the room assignment. "And according to the boss lady, this is my room. I don't suppose you were just visiting? Cuz there are two beds and three of us…"

"Ask Arthur. I do not share well." He picked me up by the lapels on my coat as if I weighed no more than a sapling. "Sir Kay called thee kin; he can keep thee." With a flick of his arm, I flew toward the bed on the south end of the room. I landed on it—and Kato—with a thud.

Mordred grabbed his ax and headed out the door. "Do not—"

"Follow you," I finished. "Yeah, yeah, I've no intention to. You were less of a Grumpelstiltzskin when I met you in

Sherwood. I don't think this therapy thing is working so well for you. Have they tried anti-brooding medication?"

No surprise, he left without answering.

"I think he's warming up to me," I said to Kato, who glared icicles underneath me.

"Whatever gave you that delusion?" he said and shoved me off.

"Well, this is the first time we've interacted that he hasn't put his ax against my throat. I'm gonna call it a win."

Kato shook his head. "That is the dark prince, the guy entirely responsible for Camelot's first downfall. And you are baiting him. What is wrong with you?"

"Too many things to list them all." Chief among them was exhaustion, which made me light-headed. Like I'd drunk dwarf-spiked punch. "Besides, aside from being all thee and thou, Mordred's not as bad as all the legends say." I picked up my crossbow and put it in the corner. "And need I remind you that all the stories and wanted posters say *we're* the bad guys who ruined all of Story? So it's like that crazy lady was saying. You can't believe what you hear cuz the winner is the only one that gets to tell their side." I took off my jacket and laid it over a chair.

Kato's jaw dropped.

"No, no, no." He picked up my crossbow and my jacket and shoved them at me. "Do not get comfy. You are not staying here. I forbid it. Go, before you fall for any more of their pixie-dusted fairy-tale cult."

He pointed at the door.

I plopped on the bed and made myself comfy. "Sorry, I don't follow commands. You are the one who's part dog, not me."

Kato looked like I'd slapped him. "A chimera is not part dog, and I just saved your life. You owe me."

"What, by calling me your cousin?" My eyelids lowered. "Yeah, hate to break it to you, but I don't think that helped any."

Roughly, Kato yanked me up and twirled me around, so I was sitting on the bed with my back against his chest.

"Look," he said.

My pulse picked up, and I squirmed to be free. "What are you—" I stopped breathing when he wrapped both arms around me.

"Look," he repeated and squeezed me still. Though he had his arms crossed, both hands were rigid, fingers fanned out. That's when I saw it. All the nails on his one hand were gone, as well as two on the other. "I realize you aren't the poster child for purity, but whatever you believe, you are still good. And a maiden. Those unicorns should have gored you before the third question."

"You stopped them with your ice and beast powers." It wasn't a question. "I thought you weren't going to help me," I said.

"You really are dense sometimes." He huffed and let go of me. "Get some sleep. You can leave tomorrow while the rest of us go to morning group. You might want to take those boots off. They've got some black gunk on them."

I laid on the bed, my thoughts weighing me down every bit as much as my body. "No can do. Your precious princess's handiwork. They're sort of rooted on."

His face instantly lightened. "You've seen her. Is she okay?"

A fragile piece somewhere in me cracked, and familiar green flecks clouded the edges of my vision. "Of course she is. Considering how tired I am, I'm guessing she's hard at work creating something useless yet high fashion. Plus, she's got Verte and a pixing Storymaker. Dorthea will be fine."

Kato smiled. "I know she will." Then he sighed. "With her practicing magic, it's the rest of Story I'm worried about."

I couldn't remember the last time I laughed hard enough for tears to brim over. Laughter is contagious as well, so Kato bowled over too, recounting all the things that had gone so wrong when Dorothea "means well."

After our guffaws died down, he tossed me a blanket. "I mean it though, Rexi. One night. Mordred is the heir to Camelot. So Excalibur is bound to come to him, one way or another."

All my mirth rotted like a worm-eaten apple as I put the pieces together. "You came here for the sword?"

"As long as Blanc has the power blockers on her wrists and neck, she can't be at full strength. She needs that sword to break their binds, so I have to find and break the sword."

And that broke my heart. It was the same story over and over. To live, I'd have to betray the people I cared about. Again.

"It really didn't matter if I'd had a thousand and one wishes. I kept trying to fill the big void I felt inside."

—Aladdin, *Rug Pulled Out from under You*

Djinn and Tonic

Luckily, I was too tired to stay awake; otherwise, I'm not sure my mind would have let me sleep. I woke up briefly when Mordred slunk back in the room and dropped his ax on the floor. When morning came, he was gone again.

"Ack. A morning person. Maybe Kato was right and he *is* evil."

While I slept in the bed with the blanket, Kato had slept on the stone floor. He jerked and whimpered in his sleep, like one of the stable master's hounds having a puppy dream. You know what they say about letting sleeping dogs lie though.

I took the blanket off the bed and placed it over him. He settled and stilled. I felt myself smiling. *No, stop that*, I told myself silently. Kato wanted me to leave so he could find the sword and destroy it. I couldn't let him do that.

Tiptoeing, I quietly grabbed my bow and slipped out of the room, then headed down the hall to explore. The corridor ended in a *T*. "Left or right." I closed my eyes. Dad had said I would be drawn to Excalibur because of the—I forgot what, but it didn't matter. If Dad thought I could find the sword like a dowsing rod, I was sure I could. Because the one thing Robin Hood never joked about was treasure.

Except I didn't feel a thing. Other than a light tapping on my leg.

"Ah," I gasped, startled to see the little emerald dragon. "Um. Good morning."

"Don't see what's particularly good about it."

"Okay, well, I'll let you work on that while I go this way." I started heading to the right.

"You're going the wrong way."

"I am?"

"Yes, group session is this way."

"Yeah." I stretched and cracked my back. "I'm not feeling that great, so I think I'll sit this one out."

Mortimer huffed. "Do you think I have nothing better to do than roam the halls fetching you? The headmistress said to make sure you were in Wish 101."

"Wish?" I put my hands up and suppressed a shudder. "Nope, no way, no how. The w-word is strictly off-limits. There's got to be another session I can go to."

"Merlin is doing a mustache-twirling intervention. I don't think you qualify."

I shook my head and crouched so I was nose to nose with him. "Look, *Sparkles*. I'm not going, and you can't make me."

"She told me you might say that." He put his little gem claws in his mouth and whistled. A whinny sounded from around the corner.

"You didn't," I said. A sneeze followed. Then a waft of glitter. I didn't wait around to find out who it came from.

Less than five minutes later, I was firmly planted in Lab Two and not a bit closer to finding Excalibur.

Gwennie stood at the front of the room, once again a vision in purple…the kind of vision that you can't stare at too long.

"Welcome, my dear ones. Let's have a pop quiz. I think everyone in here can relate to falling just shy of their goals. Do you lose to the heroes because, (A) good is stronger than evil; (B) heroes cheat; (C) they just don't make curses like they used to; or, (D) deep down, we don't think we deserve to win."

A man with a crown and dressed all in red raised his hand. It had a sock puppet on it wearing a red heart dress.

"Yes, Red King."

"What was the third one again?" he asked in a high-pitched voice, using the sock puppet to talk.

"Anyone else? No?" Gwen sighed.

"The answer is D," a voice said from the front.

Gwen smiled. "Yes. Good, Mordred. And tell us all why it's D."

I leaned over so I could see him.

He put his legs up on the chair next to him and said, "'Tis the answer that sounds the most like a load of bull—"

"Self-sabotage." Gwen cut him off. "Everyone here is guilty of spoiling plots and years' worth of machinations just as they are going right, just as opportunity is at your feet. The devil is in the details, and today I'm going to give you each an opportunity to practice getting those details right." She pulled on a curtain next to her, ripping it from the ceiling. It fell and revealed a bare-chested, chubby, bald man. Who was blue.

The other villains oohed and aahed over the genie. I really hoped it wasn't Aladdin's genie, since I had sort of recently melted his lamp in the puce cauldron acid.

Mordred stood up. "I'll go first."

"Very brave, but I believe we will start at the back." Gwen signaled the orderlies to bring up the first of the three troll bridge brothers. "One wish only, and everyone will get a turn. Wishing rules apply. No true love, no killing someone off, and no wishing for more wishes. Think very carefully about what you really want. Be careful what you wish for. And begin."

"Go, Cletus!" the elder trolls shouted.

"Aw shucks, I don't need to think. This is easy. I wish for a goat to eat." Cletus winked his one good eye at the crowd.

The genie folded his arms and bowed. "As you wish."

With a puff of smoke, Cletus was gone. In his place was a goat, not coincidentally, missing an eye, the same as the troll.

Gwen raked her nails down the chalkboard, getting

everyone's attention but scaring the goat. "You see what happened there? You must be clear and precise in your goals. Focus and believe." She pointed at the goat. "Give Cletus the tonic to undo the wish."

A straw-stuffed doll in a pink lab coat clinked beakers and tubes in the corner. "Give me a minute," an off-key voice sang. "This is precise work."

The second troll brother caught the goat...then ate him.

The trapped genie smiled a toothy, "the better to eat you" sort of grin. "He asked for a goat, and it was eaten. Wish fulfilled. Anyone else?"

After that demonstration, no one was running down the aisle for their turn. But I had an idea. I opened my mouth and raised my hand. Before I could get out words, a hand clamped across my face and dragged me backward.

"Stop this now!" Kato growled in my ear.

"Mrmrmrmr." I clawed at his wrist since I couldn't breathe. He moved his hand.

"No," I replied and stomped on his foot.

He grabbed me again, holding me tighter this time but keeping his fingers free of my nose so I could breathe. He dragged me out into the hall.

"You can't be here," he said.

"Can we just agree to disagree? You aren't going to get rid of me."

"I realize that. What I meant is you can't be *here*." He pointed toward the classroom. "See anyone you know?"

I peeked inside. "Gwen is an obvious one. I didn't know the genie personally, though he'll probably be hexed at me for wrecking his home. And I don't know the pink-lab-coat straw-voodoo doll or the blue-bearded pirate she's giving the potion to." I winced because whatever the pirate had wished for caused painful-looking gold locks to erupt all over his skin.

Kato yanked me back again. "That's not a voodoo doll. That's a *scarecrow*."

I didn't understand. "And?"

The cursed chorus of twisted voices answered instead, "*We remember.*"

A memory floated to the surface of my brain, one that wasn't mine. Instead of watching it, I relived it as if I were Dorthea.

Black Crow stood before me. Her skin turned a sallow yellow and bubbled, dripping like hot wax. One eye drooped down her cheek; the other pleaded with me. Her mouth tilted into a sickening mockery of a grin. Her limbs flattened and went boneless.

A small voice inside me rejoiced. The rest of my conscience recoiled from the monster I had become.

Black Crow's hand stretched out to me, and I rushed to it. I could fix this. Before I had a chance to help her, she slashed across my palm with a razored feather. Blood flowed freely from the almost surgical slice. I sat motionless as she applied my blood to her melting skin.

The puddling stopped, and her skin reformed into a solid state. She got a little taller and stiffer, the surface of her skin taking a clothlike appearance. Her face looked flat, like someone had painted all her features on. Her limbs got bulbous and lumpy, as though they were stuffed with straw. When the magic finished with her, what was left was not Black Crow.

What remained was a scarecrow.

Once again, I felt satisfied and horrified at what I'd done. Not to mention pity for that poor creature.

No. I refused to feel sorry for that woman. I hit my head on the doorjamb to loosen the bond and get out of Dorthea's head. Didn't need her memories. I had my own. My blood still boiled for what Black Crow has done, what she had started.

I vividly remembered being tied to a laundry line, helpless, as Black Crow made a black opal and handed it to Griz. I could never forget Griz piercing my heart and pulling out every last bit of my essence. She captured it in the opal and put the blasted necklace over her head. "If you want to live, you are going to do everything I say. You belong to me now."

"Rex," Gwen called. "It's your turn."

I hadn't worried about being recognized at Camelot, since I didn't look like my wanted posters. Neither did Kato, since the posters showed him in chimera form. And that was how Black Crow had met Kato, as the fur ball prince. But me? I knew she would remember me. Our eyes met.

Crow grabbed for a potion, and I didn't have much time. Just enough for revenge.

I rubbed my hands together. "With my wish, you're gonna see what it feels like to have someone wearing *your* soul."

"As you wish," the genie said and bowed. His smile was wider than ever.

Suddenly, my legs felt as if they were being shredded.

I screamed, collapsing to the floor as the genie yanked the boots Dorthea made off by their roots. Blood poured from the holes in my calves. With a snap of the blasted blue bastage's fingers, I was wearing Crow's pink slippers with their curled-up toes.

"Your wish has been fulfilled."

"In what possible way?" I moaned. I tried to stand, but my injured legs couldn't support my weight.

"*Perhaps you should have wished for a brain. Then you would have known* soul *has two spellings.*" Morte's voice stretched out, as did my shadow, now that I was wearing Crow's *soles*.

Be careful what you wish for, especially when the genie is holding a grudge.

Death Wish

I scooted backward until I hit the wall. I held my arms out and tried to call the Emerald flames to my palms out of instinct. A bare flicker licked across the surface.

"Fascinating," Crow said, examining me with a tilt of her head and a manic gleam in her eyes. "I had hoped to draw out the Girl of Emerald. But I suppose there are certainly a few experiments I won't mind trying on you until she finally shows herself."

She reached behind her for a bottle of liquid. I yelled, "Bow," at Kato. He hooked my dad's crossbow with his foot and lobbed it for me to snatch. Once in my hand, I fired off the closest thing I could find: the broken root shards from the boots. My aim wasn't even close to right, but the magic of the crossbow corrected it for me.

The vial exploded in Crow's gloved hand. The fabric started smoking and unraveling, until the fabric disappeared and the straw began falling out.

Crow shrieked. "The potion is not supposed to do that. My work! It's that evil girl's magic again, isn't it?" The sounds and curses Crow let out after that weren't really intelligible. She reached for bottles and started hurling them.

The other villains ran for cover, some more successfully than others. A man got hit with something yellow and turned into a lion with a scar. The hungry troll apparently thought lion was close enough to goat.

I shot makeshift bolts one after another. Kato tried to make his way to me to help, but he had to duck the shattering vials too.

"To your left."

I looked instinctually, trusting Kato. Except it wasn't Kato's voice.

My shadow was cast against the wall, and it waved its arm, even while mine stayed still. "*Welcome back.*"

Sharp pain pierced my spine, and I felt the rough scratch of straw against my neck. "Say hello to Grizelda for me." With a twist of whatever she was holding, Crow jettisoned my soul back to the underworld.

"Little hero, so nice to see you in the shade again." Morte made a motion, and before I could orient myself, copy riders scurried and swarmed me, restraining my arms and legs. "This way, if you please."

He strode out his office door into the Land of Nome Ore.

"Like I have a choice."

He looked over his shoulder and grinned with his twisted, cracked lips. "No. And you never really did."

Four copy riders carried me like a trussed-up baby deer and followed their master. The piles of Forgotten howled, but the sound wasn't as loud as I remembered it. The piles were smaller too.

In a flash, I remembered Tuck. Will. Where had they all gone?

"Rebirth," Morte answered my unspoken question simply.

"What, like they were rewritten?" I'd come back to life, so maybe Morte was sending them all back to their stories.

"Not exactly." He pointed to the fire and the forge. The ink boiled and threatened to spill over—much higher than last time.

The souls of the Forgotten…

"Oh, shh," Morte chided as I choked back a sob. "If you're quiet, you can still hear them scream." His white eyes glimmered in delight. He motioned for the copy riders to bring me to the ink trough.

I am a child of the…

"You are not a child of anything, little hero. You are nothing but an empty transport." He took his scythe quill and sucked up some of the boiling ink. "It's taken a tick longer than I'd like to make this unholy grail. But, when one has eternity, it's rather important to ensure it all gets done right. While you aren't the precise vessel I had hoped for, your untethered soul means I don't need permission to claim your undead body."

"Oh, seriously? Let me guess. You want to take over the world too?"

Morte shrugged and pushed the quill against my shin. "Not really. I'm ready to retire and relocate. Ruling is simply an added bonus. Now, hold still. This will hurt a lot."

The roots ripping out of my legs was nothing compared to Morte filling my wounds with the boiling soul ink. And he was right—I could hear them. Will. Tuck. The butcher, baker, and candlestick maker. Griz—not in the ink but by my ear.

Sssad really. You chossse the wrong sssside. Where'sss your palss now? Even Goodfellow sssold you out. You have no one.

I didn't have the strength to snark back. But Griz was wrong. I did have someone.

"Quite bothersome, you know," the genie said, hovering in the sky. He wasn't blue anymore, but olive against the Land of Nome Ore's monochromatic black and white. He wasn't chubby either, but skinny, with a salt-and-pepper mustache. He wore blue pants the princess's *Fairy Vogues* called "jeans."

Morte scowled. "What are you doing here?"

"As the beast king wishes." The jean-ie folded his arms and bowed.

The ink in my legs bubbled and spit, spilling out. Where it landed, green leaves sprouted, weaving and twisting together to grow ankle boots. The wire and parchment the copy riders held me with charred and melted together, glowing gold and adding some flourishes to the leafy footwear.

The copy riders dropped me, skittering away from the bright shine.

"Wear what you like," Morte scoffed. "You are still here. So clearly those imitation shoes lack the power of your original footwear."

The sky filled with green fire. "I am the great and powerful Storymaker of Oz," a voice boomed.

"In training!" the jean-ie interrupted.

"You ruined my entrance, Oz." The ominous voice shifted to sound like Dorthea's. "And you, King Stalker. How dare you call those shoes imitations? They're not knockoffs. They're fabulous. My finest work yet."

I didn't know whether to laugh or cry. Even unlimited power didn't change Dorthea's flair for fashion and overdramatics.

"Those boot are yours if you want them, Rexi. I'm just warning you: they're expensive."

I knew she wasn't talking about a golden goose–size charge on a Story Express card. This price tag couldn't be paid in magic beans. The moment the other boots had been yanked off, Morte had returned, but Dorthea's presence had retreated. I'd felt more myself barefoot and shooting those bolts than I had since the Sherwood Forest. She was giving me a choice. Wear the boots and live, but I'd be more tied to her than ever. Or make my own path and take on Morte alone.

Wasn't much of a choice, really. But I appreciated the attempt. Grabbing the boots, I gave them a once-over. "Did you really have to make the heels so ridiculously high?"

"Picky, picky. Just put them on and click 'em already," Dorthea snapped.

Morte howled his disagreement, clawing at me. I slipped them on and smacked them together. Morte recoiled, protecting his eyes from the golden light the boots gave off.

The escape from the underworld usually cost a memory. This time was different. I was given one of Dorthea's to relive.

I stared into a mirror held by Verte. My reflection glared with green-eyed shine, my hair crackling, sparking, hissing at its tips.

"What are you doing, Dot?" Verte asked.

"Sending a message."

"I could get a fair-e-mail," Verte offered.

"This is faster," I said to Verte. "And some sentiments can't be conveyed by a letter." Then I stared back into the mirror. "I gave you a choice. I gave you an out. You chose, and now I see you too. Remember that. Take care of what is mine, but don't ever forget he is mine. Not yours." I snapped my fingers, and the mirror cracked.

The sound of the cracking mirror matched the sounds of cracking glass in the lab as I came back to myself.

"Are you okay?" Kato hauled me off the ground.

Remembering the words of the green-eyed monster, I wiggled out of his grip as quickly as I could. Message received. "Yeah, no place like home." I rolled my eyes.

Wanted

The only ones who remained in the room were Kato, me, and the genie. The real one. And the lab was trashed. Broken glass was everywhere, and a pink pile of crushed ice and straw, which I could only assume was what was left of Crow, was scattered across the floor. I'd forgotten Kato had frost powers.

"What happened?" I asked.

The genie answered, "He made the perfect wish. An unselfish one. He wanted to know how to save you."

I saw Kato's hand before he shoved it behind his back. He'd lost another fingernail. "And to get to Dorthea, you needed to use your own power."

"I see it worked though." Kato nodded to my new boots and sighed. "She has her own way of doing things."

"Indeed she does. She's growing more powerful too, I see." Merlin stood in the doorway, beaming.

"He knows…"

"Yeah," Kato confirmed. "Somehow he knows everything. He was the one who found us in the clearing in the first place." He turned his back to Merlin and mouthed, *I don't trust him.*

Duh, I mouthed back.

Kato handed me a loop of gold.

"What's this?" I asked.

"What's left of your bow."

I stared at it horrified. "Where's the rest?"

He looked back down at my shoes, which had golden-arrow heels and gold-bow buttons. "Equivalent exchange," he said, shrugging.

"I'm going to kill her," I muttered.

"You must survive first." Merlin motioned in some orderlies. "Gwenevere demands you join her now."

The men in white coats grabbed our arms and pulled us out of the lab.

"Hey, I think we know the way by now. You can let go." They ignored me and kept marching. On the way down the hall, I saw a blur of black slip into the lab behind us. "Wait. There's—"

"Quiet," Merlin said, tapping a wand to my lips. "Touch of crazy glue. Standard use at the institution."

My mouth struggled and stretched, but it was sealed tight.

Merlin brought us to the model castle, through the door, and past the yowling kitties.

The headmistress waited in the purple room. She was looking out the window, with her back to us. "Leave them," she said in a sharp staccato.

"It might be in everyone's—particularly *my*—best interest if I stayed," Merlin answered, taking a post near the entry.

Gwen flicked her arm out, and the whip in her hand cracked and one of the crystal pieces shattered.

"Or I could just check on the rest of the patients," Merlin said.

"Good choice."

He scurried out the door. The second the door closed behind him, Gwen let out a sigh and plopped in the chair.

"Thought he was never gonna go."

I smiled as wide as my glued lips would let me, very happy

to see Hydra's crinkly face and not Gwen's smooth one. "Don' know how long I gots so best be quick."

Kato started babbling about what'd happened, but Hydra cut him off.

"Done is done. I'm not the only one who's short on time." She looked meaningfully at me. Kato looked at me too, confusion on his face. I shrugged since I couldn't say anything. "We need that steel toothpick, and we need it now." She rummaged around on her desk. "Pen. Where is that blasted pen?"

I pulled the one I'd borrowed from my coat pocket.

She took it and grabbed a piece of paper. "I'm gonna draw you a map of where it might oughta be. It's closer than a huff to a puff. I can feel it, but I've searched the whole danged desk and Merlin's workshop." She shook the pen and banged it on the paper. "This pen is still busted." She shoved it roughly back in my hand.

"Maybe somebody's already found Excalibur," Kato said.

"Nah. The only reason I'm putting up with this head is that Gwen has this lore in her bones. It's still here, or she'd know it."

Behind us, the door burst open and Merlin ran into the room. The kitties yowled. They were very efficient alarms.

"It's Mordred," he shouted over the meows.

Hydra covered her face. "Ah...ahhh choo." When she looked up, she was pure Gwen again and surprised to see us. "What is going on now?"

"After the session ended, the black prince used the genie," Merlin answered.

"And? Spit it out," Gwennie snapped.

"Mordred now wields Excalibur."

It was probably a good thing that my lips were sealed. I think curses would have flown that had never been said before. Before Black Crow recognized me, I had been about to do the exact same thing—wish to have Excalibur in my hand. I cursed her. I cursed my luck. I cursed myself because I'd lost sight of my real goal in a fit of anger and fear.

But on the bright side, at least I knew where Excalibur was. *And I am the princess of thieves. Stealing is what I do best.*

Excaliburned

Working in the Emerald palace kitchens, I'd been to dozens of balls, just never as a guest. And the party Gwenevere threw in honor of *King* Mordred that night made even Dorthea's parties look like teatime at Mother Goose's. I kept peeking at Gwen's face to see if she was Hydra, trying to make a play for the sword. But there was nary a wrinkle on her fake, smiling face. As the only girl here—well, the only girl not in disguise—Gwen was the belle of the ball. After Merlin had shared the news about the sword, Gwennie had her orderlies squeeze her into a purple eel-skin corset, which kept her middle rock solid. Unfortunately, the rest of her squished above and below and jiggled fiercely as she danced.

Filling her dance card was no easy task. Like me, none of the villains had ever been invited to a party before. Sure, they'd crashed plenty a celebration, but when you get an invitation, it's bad form to arrive and immediately start cursing the guest of honor.

The food was...interesting. Hansel, who manned the kitchens, had learned a few tricks in the gingerbread cottage. The plate labeled "ladyfingers" made me a bit nervous. One of the other institute residents, Hannibal, had no such qualms and wolfed them down. And after Rasputin slipped a little Ever-After-Clear into the punch, the party was in full swing. Puck and his band of satyrs were literally hanging from the rafters.

Kato stayed closer to Mordred than a shadow. Everyone wanted a chance to have a word or ask a favor of the returned king. I stayed in the corner of the ballroom, where, as a servant, I'd learned all the good stuff happens.

To Mordred's face, everyone bowed and said how pleased they were that Excalibur had chosen a king from the dark side of the moat. But as soon as they got out of hearing range, those same people gossiped that he wasn't a true king since he'd gotten the sword magically rather than pulling it from the stone. Maybe the title "King of the Villains" was still up for grabs.

The Knights of Knee gave Mordred a potted bush as a sign of friendship, but as they moved past me, the knights whispered that the hybrid poison-ivy plant should free up the throne by morning. And they weren't the only ones playing the game of thrones.

All over the ballroom, villains from opposite stories plotted together in groups. Dr. Jekyll had a lively conversation with the three bears in one corner, while the Headless Horseman and the Jabberwock jabbered by the grand staircase.

The unlikely pairings could've been the successful result of Gwenevere's lessons touting the importance of a healthy support system. You know, "the enemy of my enemy is... someone you can use."

That seemingly applied to friends too.

"Tag. You're it," Kato said and shoved Mordred at me. "Try to get him out of here while I head off Gwen. I think she's trying to drag him back to her room so she can be queen again."

Ew. Mental image.

I didn't ask Kato why I had to help the misogynist Mordred, (A) because my mouth was still glued shut, and (B) because Mordred had had too much punch and couldn't walk straight on his own. Which was going to make it so much easier to steal his sword and toss him into the lake.

Or maybe not. Kato let go of Mordred. He slumped on my shoulders, nearly knocking me over. I've known giants that weighed less.

"Heya. You should have this. Will put hair on thine chinny chin chin." He giggled and slammed his cup into my chest, the liquid inside sloshing up the sides. It smelled rancid and was clearly laced with something stronger than pixie dust. Probably drink of the green fairy.

I shook my head and lumbered out of the room, dragging him on my back. The lake was too far. He'd squish me before we got there. Instead, I headed down the hall to our room.

"A huntsman should be like a wolf and yer just a wee pup. Bark worse than yer bite." Mordred grinned sideways, his eyes lighting up like embers. "Ima just call thee pup."

I was tempted to drop him but settled for merely rolling my eyes hard enough that they should have fallen out. In my mind, I cursed Merlin and his stupid crazy glue and hoped it would wear off soon. Then Mordred would really hear my bark.

"A king can always use a good pup." He lowered his head to my ear. His breath smelled like a tavern. "Lemme tell thee a secret. The crown and the sword is cursed."

That got my attention. I widened my eyes, like, *Tell me more.*

"Is nay magic. Just the nature of power. 'Tis a heavy trinket and lonely. Arthur went bloody mad. Saw danger lurking under every corner." There was no correcting his clichés, as he drunkenly babbled on. "With a single stroke of a pen, our clans were labeled as traitors and threats to his perfect kingdom. He killed me mum, Morgana. And all my kin. Even me wee sister. He started a war to protect the weak, but no one protected us. I tried…" He wiped his face with his sleeve. "I'll find the grail and make it right. S'all that matters."

Once we reached the door, I tried to juggle his weight without falling face-first to the mahogany and iron rivets. Mordred tried to kick it in, but he missed. "Together. One, two, three…" We both planted our heels into the wood, and the door crashed open.

Mordred nodded at my shoes. "An odd one, you are. I like thee better when you aren't yipping. Thou art a good listener. Good pup," he said and patted the top of my head.

This seemed like the perfect opportunity to shove him off. We shuffled over to the bed, and he was snoring before he face-planted on the pillow. I stepped back and looked at the dread prince Mordred, betrayer of Camelot. Passed out, his scowl and arrogance were gone. He looked serene, helpless.

The perfect kind of mark, I could hear Dad whisper from my past.

I felt a twinge of guilt. Mordred was right, and Arthur before him. Whether you were a king or just someone who had an object of great worth, you couldn't trust anyone close to you. It was human nature to look out for number one—or to make sure you became number one.

Even sleeping, Mordred kept one hand on his ax. His coat shifted to the side and revealed his other hand resting on what I could only guess was Excalibur. He hadn't taken it out of its scabbard to show anyone its holy glow, but I recognized the fabled hilt.

Very carefully, I lifted his hand, one finger at a time, off the sapphire-encrusted handle. I tugged softly to release it from its sheath. But the sword didn't budge. Mordred had too much weight on it.

Well, hex. I wasn't going to give up, not when I was sooo close to claiming the sword and breaking the bond to Dorthea forever. Just a nudge of his shoulder…

It happened fast. I pushed and Mordred pulled, yanking me down to the bed. I thought for sure my head was about to be lopped off. Hydra would probably add it to her collection. But no. Instead of bringing the ax to me, he wrapped me up to his chest like a velveteen rabbit, murmuring something about his Beboo. Very gently, he brushed his lips across mine. It felt like a lick of fire.

Then he snored louder than before.

"Ack!" I didn't have a free hand or I would have scrubbed my lips till they fell off. I wiggled, I squiggled, I kicked and shoved, but the man was made of iron and wouldn't budge. At least I could move my mouth again and speak. Why did all spells have to involve kissing?

I thought about yelling for help but was afraid of who might answer. So I waited and waited until Kato slipped into the room. He took one look at me and covered his mouth, guffawing.

"I didn't mean to intrude. I can come back," Kato teased.

I glared hard enough I hoped it hurt him. "Very funny, fur face. Will you get me out already?"

"And you can talk again. That's too bad." He walked closer.

"I was enjoying the silence. Better tell me what happened." He crouched down and helped pry me loose.

I explained that I was trying to swipe the sword. I left out that I wasn't sure what I was going to do with it afterward.

"And then he grabbed me and…" I'd gotten loose enough at that point to wipe my lips with the back of my hand.

I expected Kato to laugh, but he paled instead. Did the kiss bother him? My pulse went up a notch. He looked away. "I'm sorry. I know how you feel."

"Huh?"

"I had to dance with Gwen to keep her from coming after you guys." Kato scrubbed at his mouth and tongue.

"Ew… How are you not…" I raised my hands up like claws and made the closest *rawr* face to a chimera's that I could.

"I wouldn't exactly call it true love's kiss." He crawled back and started helping me free again. "But still, let's keep this between us. Telling Dorthea would be a bad idea."

He is mine…

I thought of the green-eyed, blazing reflection "message" Dorthea had sent me and shuddered.

With a final yank, Kato pulled me free. I rolled off the bed and onto him in a heap. I started to push myself up, but Kato held me still. "Shhh," he whispered in one ear. Mordred grunted on the bed, feeling around for the warm "Beboo" he'd just lost.

Each grain of sand that ticked through the hourglass felt like forever. I would have much rather been cuddled to

Mordred, if only because those "get me out" feelings made a lot more sense than the jumble of emotions I felt for Kato.

Finally, he tapped me on the arm and let go. "I think we're safe. Go to sleep and let evil sleeping kings lie. We can try again tomorrow."

I didn't say anything but skulked off. My face was as red as Dorthea's heels, while Kato was cool and not the least bit self-conscious. And why should he be? I was just Rex the Huntsman. I was just one of the guys.

I looked down at the shoes Dorthea had made with loathing. These weren't rooted on, so I still had a choice to wear them or not. I took them off, tired of feeling conflicted. Shadowy tendrils crept from my feet up the moonlit wall to form the shape of a man.

"*Miss me?*"

Sick to my stomach, I crammed my feet back into the boots. Seeing Morte loom over me was upsetting—but even more upsetting was discovering that my feelings for Kato were the same whether the shoes were on or off.

"Perception is reality. If you don't like someone's reality, change their perception. Forcibly if necessary."

—Seven Habits of Highly Evil People

Pearl of Wisdom

Bad dreams and the snoring of two royal boys kept me up most of the night. No sooner had I fallen asleep than I heard my name being called.

"Rexi."

I put my pillow over my head. "Go away."

"Rexi."

I threw my pillow across the room and bolted upright. "What?!"

Both boys groaned and snorted groggily. But there was no one else in the room. I looked at my feet. Shoes were still on. Not Morte.

"Rexi!" This time the voice was impatient. And my wrist

burned. The glimmering mark of a water lily appeared. Poking my head out the window, I could see the lake and a school of jellyfish shimmering on top of the water.

I was being summoned.

Watching to make sure the boys stayed asleep, I tiptoed toward the door, keeping the gold heels from clicking on the stone floor. If I had been watching my feet, I wouldn't have tripped over an unexpected roommate.

"Oh. Don't mind me. Better to be noticed later rather than never," the little emerald dragon sniffed.

"Shhhh, you'll wake them."

"Too late," Mordred said, holding his head. "Will someone tell little boy blue to stop his bloody horn?"

Kato snorted. "I think you had a bit too much grog."

"No such thing."

While they did their guy bonding, I made my way to the exit.

"Where are you going?" Kato asked.

Stupid, nosy... "I reek. I'm, uh, going to the lake for a quick bath."

Mordred threw off his covers and sat up. "Wait for me. I shall go with you."

"No!" Kato and I shouted together.

Mordred frowned, folding his arms over his chest. "I know not what to make of you sometimes. If you two want to go bathe alone..."

"No!" we said together again.

I hoped the red in my face made me look angry not embarrassed. "I'm going. By myself. Don't follow me."

Mordred frowned. "And that's not suspicious at all."

Kato jumped in. "He sings while he bathes. Trust me, I'm doing you a favor."

"Fine," Mordred grumbled. "Keep your bloody secrets. I had no desire to spend time with you anyway." Double-checking his hips for both weapons, Mordred strode from the room, going out of his way to bump into me on the way out.

Kato sighed and rolled up to standing. "I better follow him and keep watch. All I'm gonna say is stay out of trouble."

I shrugged. "Sure. You know me."

"Which is exactly why I said it." He jogged out to catch up to Mordred.

"Ahem," the dragon coughed.

"Why are you still here?" I asked.

"The headmistress wants to see you." His jewel claws clacked on the floor. "This way."

I could have argued, but I doubt I would have won. So I wrapped the dragon in a blanket and shoved him in the closet.

"Shut that door and you declare war," he threatened.

"Sorry, but I have other plans. It could be worse. At least I didn't knock a chunk off your scales."

He sighed petulantly. "But I don't like the dark."

Yeah, I wasn't too worried. I ran to the lake as fast as I could in the heels. Getting around had gotten easier. With

Dorthea's memories and feelings, I must've acquired her useless talent for high-heeled hiking. Well, it wasn't so useless now.

"What took you so long?" the Lady of the Lake asked. The jellyfish dotted the water, but the lady was still out of sight.

"Complications. I need to leave."

"Then you have the sword?"

"No," I said slowly. "Mordred has the sword."

"Mordred. It makes sense he would find his way to it. But even if he has the sword, I can sense that Excalibur is still sleeping. It hasn't recognized him as the rightful heir to Camelot. Mordred and I have a great deal of history. Bring him to me and I will procure the sword."

"Kato is sticking to him like fish breath to the Little Mermaid. Where's my dad? We know where the sword is now; he can finish the job."

"No," the Lady of the Lake said with a ripple of waves. "Robin Hood is still a day away, and I—you don't have the time. I can feel the evil one growing stronger, and she will soon come out of hiding. You must bring Mordred alone."

Blanc getting stronger was not good news, but neither was being told that I had to trick Kato into leaving his post. So far, I'd figured that as long as I was keeping the sword away from Blanc, I wasn't betraying anyone. But actively deceiving Kato crossed a line.

"Can't do it." I put my head in my hands. "I just can't be here anymore."

Wanted

A whip of seaweed flew from the water and wrapped around my waist. I screamed for a half second before I was dragged underwater, traveling through a whirlpool until I was spit out into the lady's cave.

"Tell me what changed," she demanded, her heated voice echoing through the cold chamber. "You are dying, being destroyed and devoured from the inside by two forces that care not a whit for what happens to you. Whatever could be keeping you from saving yourself?"

Each time I went through the whirlpool, it felt like an eternity of being alone. Maybe I needed to tell someone how I felt before I exploded—or worse, broke down in tears. "Everything's messed up. I've got all these feelings. But they're for someone I can't have. So being in Camelot, close to him, is like chugging poison-apple cider."

"Rex." DumBeau stumbled around a stalagmite, tripping a few times over his Rapunzel hair-length ears. When he finally got to me, he threw his arms around me and patted the back of my head.

A sigh whipped through the chamber like a breeze. "You remind me far too much of myself for my own good," the lady said, a nearby pool of water growing into the shape of a see-through woman. "I too once loved a man who I wasn't supposed to have. He loved me as well. And that angered the supposed heroine of the story."

I squirmed to get out of DumBeau's well-meaning but crushing embrace. A few minutes ago, I would have said the lady was lying about someone falling in love with her, but the woman made of water was a far cry better to look at than the jellyfish, kelp, and eel swamp thing. Still, her story didn't add up.

"Wait. I was raised on the legends of Camelot. And that wasn't in any of the stories."

The liquid sculpted more, further defining the woman's details.

"Haven't you learned by now that every story has more than one version?" The nearest pool of water shimmered, showing an image of my friends and my outlaw posters in succession. There was a new line at the bottom of the poster: Dead or Alive. *Great.*

"So what's the unauthorized version?"

"I tried to be nice and follow the rules. I thought that love would conquer all. I was wrong. The heroine decided if she couldn't have him, then no one should. So she ordered Morgana La Fey to create a death curse."

"Is that what happened to Mordred? Or was it Arthur?" I racked my swiss cheese memory. "Who was he, and what happened to him?"

Water beads formed on the rocks overhead. *Drip. Drop.* It was as if the cave were crying. "My dearest love died in my waters, and that is why he is known in all the versions of the story as Lancelot de Lac. Lancelot of the Lake."

Drip. Drip.

After all these centuries, the Lady of the Lake still mourned

Lancelot. And if I put her story alongside the "official" legend, it wasn't hard to figure out who the other woman, the heroine, was—Gwenevere.

"And then there is your story, an echo of my own," the lady started.

There was a distant splash, and DumBeau perked up.

"It's Kato," the Lady of the Lake said.

I sighed. "Yes, I know. It's complicated and I couldn't have picked a worse person to fall for, but it's not like I could help it."

"No, I meant it's Kato in my lake, looking for you." The drips slowed. "He cares for you, so perhaps your situation is less complicated than you think. Take the sword and fight. No one, no matter their story, is unworthy of being loved. You deserve this happiness."

"I can't. Betraying him would kill me faster than Dorthea or Morte or any of Gwennie's self-empowerment therapies. I just can't go back to Camelot again."

Every puddle and pool of standing water boiled. "Gwenevere. She's alive? And holds Camelot?"

"Well, sort of. I mean her head does. Not sure where the rest of her went."

"It's ash. Her body was burned at the stake after Arthur beheaded her for treason and what she did to me." The lady's body exploded into millions of droplets and whipped through the cavern like a squall. "If Gwenevere is in Camelot, Mic must have succumbed to her charms. She will try to seduce Mordred next and claim Excalibur. We have to be ready."

"Mic...as in the Mimicman? Whoa." The seaweed struck out at me again, this time grabbing my heels and snapping off their golden arrows.

"I need these, but I give you this pearl in exchange." A glistening orb floated up out of the water. "Magic can create but a pale imitation of love. However, it can give you a fair shot. Put this in Kato's mouth and he will forget all before him except you. Beyond that, securing his love is something only you can do. But if you don't go now, I believe he will drown searching for you."

"Stay, Rex." DumBeau plucked the pearl from the pool and laid it in my hand, then threw me in the whirlpool. "Away."

The watery cyclone tossed and turned me before spitting me back out. Kato was not on the shore. I looked to the lake. I could see a black shape splashing, then sinking.

Without a thought, I dove back in. *What was he thinking? Jumping into a lake in a full suit of armor?* The whirlpool had disappeared, meaning Kato was sinking to the bottom of the lake. He couldn't breathe underwater like I could.

I grabbed Kato and furiously kicked my way back to the surface.

"You moron," I cursed, dragging him to shore and pulling off his armor so I could get to his chest. No heartbeat. "You can't have him, Morte!" I pushed on Kato's chest again and again. He wasn't breathing. I was about to blow air into his lungs when he started coughing up water like a fountain.

I pushed him onto this side so that he could breathe. Then I thumped his back, perhaps a smidge harder than necessary. "What were you thinking?"

"From the castle. Saw you. Fall into lake." He sputtered and hacked more.

"I'm immortal, you big beast. You, on the other hand, are not."

"I don't like it when you suffer or die. You come back different, and I don't want you to go through that. I can't watch the embers of your life's hearth fade." He huffed and closed his eyes. "You are important to me, so I'm going to take care of you. Deal with it."

The pearl in my fist grew hot.

I could use the enchantment. Just a quick pop, like a pill. It would be so easy. Why shouldn't I get a chance? Maybe he could love me if he didn't have *Dorthea* on his mind.

As soon as the thought came, I pushed it away. I was ashamed I'd even considered it. I knew what it was like to be controlled, to lose a piece of myself. I would never wish that upon anyone. Let alone someone I—

I felt her a split second before the strike of lightning cracked the ground. A dust cloud formed from the damage, but the outline of a figure was plainly there.

Kato eased himself up and squinted to see what was going on. "Who's that?"

"The lightning was green."

We both gulped as the dust filtered away.

Dorthea's hair was fully alight and crackling as she walked toward us slowly, purposefully placing each step. Every time her foot hit the ground, the grass would wither and die, leaving a yellow road of destruction in her wake.

"I warned you," she said.

We have come for you. We have come for you all, the curse added louder than ever. The chorus of voices had grown in number.

I pushed Kato away just before the flames consumed me.

28

The Ex-Factor

All is one and one is all.

The curse's fire seared my veins, coursing through me. All the while, the chorus spoke to me, whispering of what used to be. Of what is. Of what will be. The fire showed me visions. They didn't feel like memories, just images that made no sense. A baby. A weeping red tree. A twin-tailed black beast. A mirror with Blanc's reflection. A flower. A white room filled with boxes that beeped. A sleeping girl. A book. A headstone.

When I opened my eyes, the flames were gone. So was the lake. And Kato. And Dorthea. Somehow I was sitting in Camelot's library. Gwen and Merlin were bickering about how to formally set tea upon a triangular table. The silver teapot mocked me. My reflection showed a hollow-eyed girl with short, blond spikes. It was me and not me. Rexi. I didn't recognize her anymore.

Before I forgot, I grabbed the pen from my coat pocket and rolled up my sleeve. The black marks slashed across my skin told me a story I didn't want to believe. Thirteen. I searched my memories, but they skipped and jumped between past and present, between my experiences and Dorthea's. I didn't remember dying the last three times. I remembered being murdered by Crow. After that, there was a memory of death, but neither the recollection nor fatality were mine.

If I recalled the chorus of the damned, I'm positive I heard the scarred chimera, Griff, hissing at me. I spoke my suspicions out loud. "Dorthea used the curse to kill the chimera traitors."

"Yes. After we left the forest, we took refuge with Bobbledandrophous to finish training. Blanc's rogue chimeras ambushed us, and Dorthea lost control," Verte said, settling herself down beside me. "What happened to you? You look like plankton that Monstro the whale spit out."

"Thanks."

"And there's only one way you would know about those nasty beasts." Getting far too close, she opened my mouth and breathed in. She clucked, her green, crooked nose crinkling. "You didn't take your medicine like I told you to. Sure, I've lived a few hundred years, but no, of course you know better than me. What was it? Couldn't find a spoonful of sugar to make the medicine go down?"

"A handshake with Captain Hook went horribly wrong." I shrugged. "So what are we doing here? Is this a tea intervention or something?"

"Or domething," Gwen said. No, not Gwen. Hydra. She had a clamp on her nose and had even grown an age spot. She pointed to clamp. "Godoo keep from dneezing. Gwen cand be allowed oud near Dordea."

"And where is her royal roastiness?"

"In the other room. We are trying to use Kato's frost powers to chill her the spell out." Verte sighed. "Out of all the boys in Story… I knew you were likely to end up here, but I didn't foresee this bippidy backfire."

"It is exactly what it should be," Merlin said, taking a seat at the apex of the triangle. "I will take charge of the Girl of Emerald from now on."

Verte and Hydra both started talking at the same time.

"Wasdn' dis dable round? I apifically rebeber id being round."

"What sort of newt-brained idea is that?"

The three of them bickered about what to do next. I wanted no part of it. I had enough internal bickering going on. The longer I was awake, the more I got a handle on the situation. The library had stacks and stacks of musty books and scrolls. There was a cauldron in the corner and an owl sitting on a perch. Upon seeing the little gold hat the owl wore, I remembered something the Lady of the Lake had said.

"That's not Merlin."

The three kept arguing over me. I slapped my palm on the

table. It crackled and sizzled, leaving a charred palm imprint on the wooden surface. Everyone stilled. "I said, that is not Merlin. That is the Mimicman."

"Pish," Verte dismissed. "You've been tapping into Dot's madness and paranoia. There's not a speck of that gaudy gold on him. And look." She grabbed him by the beard and shoved his face toward the teapot. "Same reflection."

She was right. About those two points at least. "How do we know that rule didn't mend itself? You recognized me as a girl while everyone assumed I was a boy," I said to Merlin.

"That's easily explained, as I am a simply a great lover of women." He swatted at Verte. "Get your gangrenous hands off me, you bitter old hag," he said, then coughed, straightening up with a pleasant face. "Think about this logically. I came to you for help once Blanc took over Camelot with the villains. Would this Magnificent Mimicman do that?"

I was right. I had to be. Everything added up. I looked at my hand, the slight green smoke wafting off it, and felt the smile on my face.

"What are you doing?" he asked, standing and tripping over his chair as he retreated a few steps.

If I focused, I could see the lines of power running through everything—magical essence that fueled all living and enchanted beings and items. So far I'd gotten the crispy end of the curse, but perhaps that was just because I'd been running away and hadn't been willing to embrace it. I narrowed my eyes and honed in on the trail of power around him. And

I tugged on one of the lines I could see while I borrowed Dorthea's magic.

I could feel the Emerald curse waking, a grumble thinking of its next meal.

Merlin's face went slack. "What are you doing? Stop."

"Blast it all. Now we've got two of 'em." Verte grabbed the teapot and held it like a weapon.

I looked her straight in the eye. "Trust me."

She hesitated, then lowered it.

"Are you mad?" Merlin turned to Hydra and tried to pull the clamp off her nose. "Help me, Gwenevere."

"Dope."

I pulled and wound the power around my hand like a string. There were two lines. One, a thin, gold thread. The other was a thick braid of life magic. The curse was interested in devouring Merlin's life. I only wanted to disrupt the magic of his glamour. With a final tug, the gold thread snapped.

Merlin gasped and shuddered. He fell to the ground, writhing. For half a second, I thought I'd killed him. Then, fur started spouting all over his body, big black wings grew out of his back, and golden horns twisted from his skull.

"Um. Okay. That I was not expecting," I said, backing up from the giant chimera. His lion's body was twice the height and width of Kato's. And Kato's dragon tail didn't have barbs.

"We figured it out during the hollabaloo in the mountain with Griz. You were living impaired at that moment." Verte raised the teapot again, but not at me. "Rexi, meet

Bestiamimickos. Also known as the First Beast King, Wizard of Is, Mic the Mimicman, and the most self-absorbed man with a Peter Pan complex that has ever been written, and I woulda coulda shoulda erased him from the page ages ago."

"All this just because I mimicked your hideous form," Mic growled. "You don't know me. You don't know the pain I've suffered or love I've los—ow." His pity party ended when the teapot bopped him on the nose and bounced off, getting stuck on his horn.

"Dow he's done id."

The emerald eye in Verte's belt clouded over, not in the "foretelling a prophecy" way, but as if a hurricane were imminent.

"Don't know you, ya say." She flicked her wrist, and a book flew off the shelf and pelted the large chimera in the side. "You trip trap tiptoed around me for years." Smack. Another book flew at the chimera. "Begged me to look beyond your shedding problem." And another. "Then you took up with that soggy psycho Blanc and started a war. But you wanted forgiveness." This time the whole row of *Magipedia Brittanica* flew at him, knocking him over with a thud. "You swore. You said you'd spend an eternity doing good to make up for all your damage." *Whack* "You." *Whack.* "Caused." *Whack.*

"How would you know that?" the beast grumbled.

"Becud she wad dere, idgid."

"No. The only people there when I made that promise were Blanc, the Storymaker, and my beloved Dorthea, the first Princess of Emerald." After he let that sink in, Mic shook his head, fur flying off his mane. "No. Inconceivable. My princess was beautiful and kind. And human. Nothing like this rotting, green wretch covered in warts."

Watching Verte throw books and berate Mic, I could totally see the Emerald temper family resemblance.

"It's been nearly three hundred years. Some of us age more gracefully than others. And you can blame Frank for the ozification of my skin." The hair in Verte's warts grew longer and curlier as if to spite the man. "I've watched over generations of the House of Emerald, biding my time and working until all my pieces and plots were in place to end this saga once and for all. And you and your philandering, over-chemically, hormonified beastliness has been chasing after a girl one-fiftieth your age. You should be ashamed."

"You should be dead," Dorthea said. Her flat voice put a bigger chill through my bones than her anger ever had. Through the bond, I should have known she was behind me before I heard her, but I was too wrapped up in the carriage wreck in front of me.

"Simmer down, sapling," Verte said, motioning Kato to get Dorthea out of the room. "I can handle this pox on my own."

Dorthea shook her head, the flames of her hair burning eerily stable—not snapping or popping, but bright and calm. Her eyes were blank as she called the Emerald curse along the tips of her fingers. "If you were handling this properly, he wouldn't be breathing. But I can fix that."

"Strong people don't put others down; they lift them up. Makes the fall that much more satisfying."

—Red Queen, *Lots of Heart: How to Get a Head*

29

Might Makes Right

Dorthea flipped her hand and Mic doubled over. No one else could see what she was doing except me, because I could see the lines of power. She was burning the braided lifeline.

Kato tried to get close to her, but Merlin's owl flew from its perch and barreled into his chest. Anyone who touched Dorthea right now would be a nice snack for the Emerald curse. Last time I'd touched her, I'd nearly been eaten alive, the curse taking over me.

And now I was going to do it on purpose.

After jumping in front of Dorthea, I felt the Emerald power pull at me. This time, I pulled back. Dorthea still wore my opal, but it didn't resemble a fire opal anymore. It was mystic green with swirls of black and only tiny hints of a red-orange glow.

"Let go," she said. "Don't you remember what Mic did to me? What he's done to countless stories?"

"Memory isn't my specialty right now." I grunted because the struggle had gotten harder. "But ask yourself if you really want this slimeball crawling around in your brain."

She paused her power draw for a second. But that was all I needed. "I vote no, since we have to share our minds. So thanks for the power loan, but here, have it back." I didn't want to drain Dorthea's power—I wanted to overload her. I pushed everything I had into her. She gasped, her eyes rolling back in her head.

Kato caught Dorthea as she crumpled to the ground, out cold.

Mic was down for the count but breathing.

I swayed and fought to stay on my feet. The green opal on Dorthea's chest had darkened, and a crack was webbing out from its center.

Verte walked over to Mic and snorted. Then hawked a very unladylike loogie on the passed-out Beast King.

"Eww." I scrunched my nose. Mic wasn't the only one having a hard time reconciling Verte with some ancient, dainty princess.

Beside me, the owl started hacking and gagging too.

"Seriously?" I pointed to the chimera. "If you've got an issue with your boss, take it up with him but don't upchuck over here."

The owl didn't listen. It barfed out a mouse. Ish. Even covered in slime, I could see the mouse was half-mini-rhino. With a puff of smoke, the rhimouserous changed into the stuffy old man in the tweed jacket.

"Sorry I'm late. I'm afraid I've been rather occupied," Oz said, combing the slime out of his mustache. "Thank you for the hospitality, Nikko, you can go," he said and shooed away the owl.

"Bah, just when we knock out one old fool, another pops up." Verte hobbled over to Oz and poked him in the gut. "You can't fool me. I know you were tick-tocking the seconds to make the flashiest entrance you could."

He wiped the sludge off his glasses next. "Not at all. I simply waited until most of the danger had passed."

I rolled my eyes. "I forgot you Storymakers like to control the action with your pens from a safe distance."

Oz blinked. "Of course. If one gets too close to the story and the lives of the people in it, well, it makes it that much harder to do what needs to be done."

Verte glared, poking harder. "And what, in your meddling opinion, needs to be done?"

"I think you know exactly." He stared pointedly at Dorthea. "There is a very good reason that Storymakers can't linger in this realm. If you want to preserve Libraria as it is, you need to banish her to the other world."

"No," Kato said firmly. "You're here. You're a Storymaker, so surely there must be something that can be done."

Oz wiggled his mustache thoughtfully. "I doubt you'd wish my fate on her." He reached into his pants' pocket and pulled out a square. After dusting it off, he blew into one corner until the square was thick and rectangular. "There." With a final tap, he was holding *The Book of Making* that we had taken back from Griz.

"Okay, we have all almost died—"

"Speak for yourself," I interrupted.

Kato continued. "All right, some of us have died for that book. What is it?"

"A work in progress," Oz answered simply.

"Yeah, that makes total sense," I said, sitting down and fiddling with my pen.

Oz brightened and nodded to me. "Oh good. I was worried. Most people don't understand the pen being mightier than the sword theology."

He flipped open the book. The illustrations moved, like watching one of the mirror pads they had at the Emerald Palace, not that I ever got to mess with them in the kitchens. But I'd seen them. He flipped through the pages. Blanc appeared on the early pages. Then the chimera prison.

Verte craned to get a peek. "Oooh, I looked good." She pointed at a girl with brown hair and a crown who was standing off against Blanc.

Kato and I gave each other a look that said more than words ever could. If we didn't want to be turned into toads, silence was the best course.

Oz skipped farther ahead.

"Hey, wait. What's in those chapters?" I asked.

Oz narrowed his eyes and peered down his nose. "Spoilers." He flipped forward to a page that showed Queen Em and King Henry. They were arguing in a white hallway. But they wore strange clothes and were without their crowns. "Now this is the world of the Storymakers. This is where we need to—"

There were dual growls overruling the Storymaker, one from the freshly awakened former Beast King, Mic, and the current Beast King, Kato.

Oz grumbled. "What is it with you chimeras and Emerald women?"

"The princess is currently the most powerful being in Story," Mic said.

Kato snorted, stealing my response. "She's not a *being*. She's Dot."

I finished his thought. "And how could you possibly say that with a straight face when we are in the room with a Storymaker? And whatever Hydra is. Plus, there's the Emerald Sorceress, Dorthea's great-great-great-great-great—"

"We get the point," Verte muttered.

"—great-great-granny. Surely one of you has more oomph than a shoe-obsessed girl," I finished.

The room was silent.

"We's doobed." Hydra buried her face.

"Surely she's not stronger than Blanc?" I questioned.

Mic sniffed. "While the White Empress still has the

binds we placed on her, my princess, Dorthea, is at least doubly powerful."

"Which makes her doubly as dangerous too," Oz pointed out. "Right now, she is out of balance. Very few have the gift of a Storymaker, to both give and take life. And Dorthea can actually create it. Blanc could never do that. The water sorceress is adept at taking life and has somehow figured out she can return life to a select few."

I remembered the *Compendium of Storybook Characters*, the names being whited out. "That's where the influx of villains and legends came from."

"She's building an army," Mic said. "After I fled the mountain, I knew she would come for Excalibur and use Camelot and the grail to continue the war. That's why I stole the sword and came here first. But as soon as I entered the castle, the sword vanished."

"And so you cowered here like the yellow-bellied toad you always were, hiding while Blanc brought back the worst of the worst." Verte looked like she was going to spit again.

"Your attitude has grown as ugly as your face, Verte," Mic sneered. "I could have changed into any number of faces and stayed out of the entire affair, but no. I stayed in the center of it all and warned you, sent for you, and didn't sell you out in your little hideout."

Oz scratched his nose. "He has a point."

Verte harrumphed and shut up. As it had been ever since

Blanc went free, the difference between good and evil, villain and hero, was clear as obsidian.

"What about the sword?" I asked. "We know where it is now. Could Excalibur stop the Emerald curse?"

Oz flipped through the book, hiding the pages. Kato perked up for a moment, then looked darker than ever as Hydra shook her head.

"Nod widoud killing her," Hydra answered.

My insides turned colder than if Kato had frozen me on the spot. Both Dad and the Lady of the Lake had left out that part. So this was the truth of the whole thing. From the moment Griz had sealed my life into the opal, if I wanted to live, Dorthea had to die.

"My princess needs the grail." Mic finally stood on all four paws. His golden horns brushed the ceiling.

Kato hit the table with his fist, cracking it down the center. "There has to be another answer. Dorthea's only chance at life cannot be a mythical artifact that no one's ever seen or been able to find."

"I've seen it." Mic breathed in deeply. As he inhaled, his body shrank, and his horns, hair, tail, and wings receded. Suddenly, he looked like Merlin again. "And the reason why no one can find the grail is because it was locked away while its owner was asleep."

Oz's bushy eyebrows rose like hairy caterpillars. "Aha. That's how she's been bringing people back into the story. Blanc is using the grail. Well, that solves that mystery."

The sparkly green dust started to rise around him. Kato grabbed Oz by the coat before he could change into something else.

"No. You aren't leaving this time." He dragged Oz over to Dorthea. "You are going to stay put and keep her safe while we go get the grail." He turned to Mic. "Tell me where it is."

"And let you have the glory of saving my love?" He threw his head back and laughed. "Not likely. I will go and retrieve it."

The two chimeras growled in their human forms and circled the table. Green flames licked my hands as I slammed them into the triangle table again. "Knock it off. You are both going to go play fetch, and I am going to keep you from peeing on each other to prove who loves Dorky more."

Both men looked down and grumbled but didn't object.

Verte pointed her red, razor nails my way. "You've changed." Her belt clouded white and she nodded. "Good. You're nearly ready."

"For what? You make it sound like I'm a muffin in the oven."

Verte winked. "Huh? What was that? I'm getting senile, since I'm a great-great-great-great—"

Knowing she'd only tell me when she was good and ready, I huffed and stormed out, waving behind me as I did. Mic and Kato followed. We made it partway down the hall before Mordred stepped out of the shadows.

Wanted

"Can't play right now," I said, shooing him off.

"I truly am sorry, but this might hurt thee worse than me." He grabbed my wrist and whipped me around, holding a sword at my throat. "Take me to the grail."

30

I've Got an Eye on You

N o." Mic turned the other direction.

Kato grabbed him. "Wait."

Mic huffed and shrugged. "Rexi is dead anyway. Focus on the one that matters."

"They both matter."

Mic poked Kato in his shoulder. "And that, pup, is why you will lose. You can't save them all."

"Pardon me?" Mordred said. "Remember us?"

I stomped on his foot with my broken heel and bit his wrist, freeing his grip on me and the sword.

I swiped his sword, finally doing what I'd come to Camelot for in the first place. Not exactly stealth, but it didn't matter if

Mordred knew I had Excalibur as long as I was faster. "I can save myself, thanks," I snarked at the guys as I sprinted past.

I didn't make it very far before a row of orderlies blocked my path. Sparkles stood in front of them. "You should have left the light on for me. I really do hate the dark. This means war." He opened his mouth, and that horrific, high-pitched alarm came out.

Kato grabbed my hand, and we pivoted. "Hurry."

The urgency was even more pressing once we got outside. Gwennie's little nightmares had been released. Cute and glitter-shedding teacup unicorns galloped across the field one minute, flame-snorting demons ran across it the next. When they got closer to the castle, they slowed. They sensed the same shift in the air I did. There was a powerful maiden inside. And she was waking up.

"This way." I was still holding Kato's hand and dragged him behind the castle while the mini-night-mares were confused. We doubled back to Gwen's model castle. Mic followed behind us and barred the doors. We'd lost Mordred and the lethal unicorns—for now. But if the crystal kittens kept yowling…

Mic transformed just his chimera tail and took out the entire hutch in one sparkly catastrophe.

"There. I've wanted to do that since the moment Gwenevere arrived," Mic wheezed. "You know I sent you that fair-e-mail so you would come here and keep me safe. For supposed heroes, you're rather bad at this rescue business."

"It's not over," Kato said. "We're not dead yet."

"That could change at any minute. She's awake and—ow!" I flinched as heat seared the mark on my wrist. Kato quickly let go of my hand with an apology.

"It's not you," I assured him. "But is there any way we can see what's going on with Dorthea?" I had a really bad feeling.

"There's an eyepod in the desk." Mic threw open a drawer and started chucking all the clutter. There was enough makeup and girly stuff that even Dorthea would drool. They didn't exactly match the other half of the contents, which looked like mid-evil torture devices. Finally he pulled out a purple crystal ball—with an eye carved in it.

As soon as Mic set it down on the desk, it rolled around, looking at each of us as if it were alive. "That's a lot like…"

"That green goblin's belt. Yes, don't remind me." Mic frowned, still apparently upset to be reunited with his ex, Verte.

Kato ignored him and kept talking. "If Verte's emerald belt is related to the Pendragons and Camelot, then all our story lines are tied in a much closer knot than I ever thought."

"I thought Legends and Fairy Tales weren't supposed to tangle." I'd grown up in the forest that straddled the two realms, and until Dorthea's wish, I'd never known them to mix.

"Libraria was different before the empress fell," Mic said.

Oz's voice came from the eye as the amethyst turned cloudy. "And in this realm, every action, every deed is interconnected. If a fairy dies in Neverland, the effect will be felt all the way in Emerald. Everyone matters. Every decision changes the course of a story."

"Wait, wait, wait." I cocked my hip and slapped my hand on it. "How can you say that as a Storymaker? One's fate is written the way it is. And nothing can change that."

"Pfft. Hog-wart wash. Stories are living tales. They are always growing and changing." The crystal resonated, like someone whacking it.

"Leave my belt alone, old coot," Verte said, but it was Oz's face that suddenly appeared close up in the eyepod.

"Can you see me now?" he asked.

Verte's hand entered the picture, pushing Oz away. "Back up, or the only thing they're gonna see is up your nose."

I held the sword up to the amethyst, unsure if the picture was two-way. "We got waylaid. But tell Dorthea I have Excalibur, so Blanc's not going to get her hands on it."

"I can hear you just fine," Dorthea said, her voice low.

"Now back to what I was teaching you." Oz grabbed a book off the shelf. *SCUBA: The Singing Crustacean's Underwater Ballroom in Atlantis.* He flipped it open to a page that showed a little, red crab directing an orchestra for one of King Neptune's parties.

Dorthea dug her nails into the broken table. "Get to the point."

"Waid for id," Hydra said.

No sooner had she said that than the picture started to disappear. Like a watercolor left out in the rain, the image faded to nothing.

"Why did it do that? What does it mean?" I asked.

Oz took off his glasses, breathed on them, then wiped them clean. "It means that this story is changing. What you saw is no longer what happens."

Now Dorthea was interested. She took the book and flipped through the pages. They were all empty. "What happened to the crustaceans?"

Putting his glasses back on, Oz looked perfectly unconcerned as he said, "They've been erased."

Gone. In just a few moments. How many characters…gone?

"She's reclaiming the water," Mic said quietly.

No one needed any elaboration on who *she* was.

Dorthea frantically flipped through the book. Some of the pages still had images, but they were fading fast. She flipped to one where the illustration stayed static. But I wished it hadn't. King Neptune was slumped in his throne, a golden arrow in his chest. It was the same arrow that the Lady of the Lake had taken from me.

No. No. No. Please no. Not again. I didn't…

Dorthea pointed to the symbol engraved into the pillar next to him. "She's mocking me, leaving a calling card saying come get me. Wish granted."

Oz peered closer at the symbol. "The lotus rose. I've seen that somewhere… There are too many pieces in my head."

The book was too difficult for us to see through the eyepod, but I had a feeling I knew exactly what that flower looked like. And why Oz had déjà vu again.

I stared at my wrist. There was nothing there now, but I

knew what shimmered beneath the skin. I'd been marked with that same flower symbol by the Lady of the Lake, Blanc. The pieces snapped into place. The "service" I had done for her—aiding Griz in retrieving the spring water that eventually set her free.

I dug my nails into my wrist of the other hand, hard enough to draw blood and stop my hands from shaking. Why was it, no matter how hard I tried, I always ended up back in the same place? On the wrong side.

"What are you doing?" Kato asked.

"Nothing." I rubbed my eyes and shoved my hands in my coat. He couldn't know Blanc made me her champion. *Please don't let him ever know.*

"Lesson's over," Dorthea said and slammed the book closed. She whipped out her grimmoire. As she was without a pen, she lit her finger and burned her words into the pages. "This. Ends. Now."

With a flurry, pieces of the chair and books whipped around, reforming into a red umbrella. She pointed her finger at the library chimney, and green flames erupted there. After adding a few more notes to her pages, she popped open her umbrella and flew up the flue. As she disappeared, the chimney flames fanned out, consuming the room. The amethyst eyepod cracked and went purple again.

Kato hit it repeatedly, cursing the thing to come back online.

"She's going to die," Mic said and stumbled into a chair. "We're all going to die."

Wanted

"I thought you said she was more powerful than Blanc," Kato snapped, throwing the broken ball at Mic.

"Fire cannot win under the water. Magical umbrella or not."

"And that witch has Neptune's trident," I added. "She didn't go after Atlantis just to wipe it out. She went to free her binds."

Mic quirked an eyebrow at me but didn't question it. He'd felt the mark when he'd grabbed my wrist at Gwen's the first time. He knew.

All at once, a blinding pain seared my mind.

Kato rushed to my side, helping me to the ground before I toppled. "What's wrong?"

I couldn't answer, but I didn't need to since Mic seemed to understand. "Our warrior princess is traveling to Atlantis using this girl's life force as a force field. It won't be enough though. The empress will have closed the whirlpools, locking down the city."

"So Rexi and Dorthea…"

"Yes, they'll both be dead before Dorthea ever gets to Blanc."

31

Other True Love's Kiss

Kato roared his human throat hoarse. When he finished, he shoved his finger in his mouth and ripped the nail off his ring finger.

He cradled my head in his hands, and I could feel myself getting stronger.

"Please, Rexi. I'm going to go bring her back. Hang on for both of you until I do."

"Didn't you hear me, mutt?" Mic sneered. "There's not enough time. And there's no way we can get past those hexed night terrors and make it to the water."

"If you loved Dot like you say, you'd try," Kato yelled back.

They argued, helping no one. Not Dorthea. Not the others

in the burning library. Mic grew angry and shuddered, changing to his true form.

"How dare you challenge your progenitor?"

That was it. I knew what to do. "Kato, you have to fly," I said.

He looked at me, crestfallen. "If I use the last nail for power, I'll die. And I can't change at will like this one can."

"Ah yes, your ability to change is tied to that magic-kiss nonsense." Mic scrunched up his muzzle in condescension. "But Rexi's right. Flying, we might make it. But we have to go now. Hurry and kiss her already."

"For being magical, you are a narcissistic nimrod. It has to be true love's kiss," Kato argued, his chest rising and falling. "Gwen kissed me and nothing happened."

Mic looked at me. Really, more like looked into me.

"Oh, be a beast already, and do it." Mic swiped his tail across the floor, knocking Kato off his feet, then spun him around so he rammed into me.

Kato opened his mouth to say something, but I didn't let him. I pulled him close before I chickened out.

I'd already lived this moment once, through Dorthea's memory. That memory couldn't compete with the real thing. It didn't matter where Dorthea ended and I began; in that moment, Kato was kissing *me*. His hand cupped my chin. His lips pushed against mine. And then it was over. I didn't want to open my eyes. I didn't want my once upon a time proved to be an illusion.

"Oh, Rexi," Kato said. His voice was gruff, and I knew our kiss had worked. "Look at me," he commanded.

I obeyed, letting his eyes search mine for some explanation, some loophole to the rule. When he found his answer, saw the truth, he bowed his furry head against mine. "I'm sorry."

I hadn't expected a different reaction, but my heart shattered anyway. I forced the corner of my wavering lips to turn up.

"S'okay. Go," I croaked out.

Kato nodded and bounded up, breaking through the roof and flying off to save his princess.

Mic padded over to me, a mix of pity and disgust telegraphed across his muzzle. "I don't understand you. I protected you so you could tear him away from her. When you were drained, I saw that pearl in your pocket. Why didn't you use it? You'd have to be blind as a mouse not to see there is chemistry between you two."

"If I won his love that way, with the pearl, I wouldn't deserve it."

Mic shook his head. "You are either far too wise or too foolish to live." He crouched on his haunches and then sprang up into the sky after Kato.

The extra life magic Kato pushed into me was helping, but Dorthea was draining it faster than it could replenish.

"Seriously," I muttered to myself. "She spent how long shrieking at the hint of a sprinkle of rain and now she goes and jumps in a lake?"

Groaning, I rolled over and spotted the sword. "I may not be able to fly, but I bet those glitter-poxed ponies will think twice before tangling with Excalibur."

"Pssst," a voice called from the window. "Are they gone?"

"Good timing," I said as Robin Hood jimmied open the lock and slipped inside. "You do realize the whole roof is open."

He shrugged, shooting me a grin. "Where's the challenge in that?" Looking down at the treasure I held, he whistled long and low. "Is that what I think it is?"

"In the steel."

I gasped as another wave of power drained out of me. Dad picked up the sword as if it were made of delicate glass.

"Wait, whatever you were planning on doing, you can't. The Lady of the Lake is Blanc. And she's in Atlantis stealing the trident. And Verte said that whoever uses the sword to break the curse and bond will kill Dorthea. Which is exactly what Blanc wants, so we have to make sure that doesn't happen." I was gasping by the end.

"I made a promise." He nudged my boots. "The situation has changed, it seems, but I am a man of my oaths. And I swore to get these off you."

The power drain was coming faster, making it hard to move. I couldn't catch my breath. I tried to keep Dad from taking off my boots, but in the end, he slid them off with ease. Inky blackness spilled out, puddling and spreading beneath me.

"Ahh. Thank you. It was getting cramped in there."

Wanted

"As a gesture of goodwill, I offer you a trade," Robin said.

"*I'm listening*," said Morte.

I tried to warn Dad not to make any sort of deal, that it wasn't worth it, but I was still weak—and too surprised that he could also see and hear Morte.

"It seems the empress no longer needs the sword, so I will give it to you if you call our debt square." He gestured toward the shoes. "And I get to keep the shoes as insurance."

"Dad?" I tried to see the con, the angle. The only one I could come up with was him double-crossing me. "You can't do this."

"It's the rogue's code: rob from the rich; give to the poor. Or sell to the highest bidder." Robin raised his pant leg. He too had black rings around his ankle. If he owed Morte a debt, that meant he'd died and come back.

"*Yes*," Morte answered my thought. "*Blanc erased your father's name from the compendium. But everyone knows that the only two truly unavoidable events in this world are death and paper cuts.*"

Robin Hood disagreed. "Not if we have a deal. I give you Excalibur, and you cannot recall me to the underworld, ever."

"*Deal. Keep the sword safe for me in the forest until I ascend. Oh, and I will need this little hero's body. Is that going to be a problem?*"

Dad looked at me, his rakish smile gone, but I couldn't read the expression on his face. "You do what you have to, to survive."

Morte chuckled darkly. "*We have an accord. I shall finish the preparations.*" The monstrous shadow shrank beneath me.

Dad turned to leave, shoes and sword tucked under his arm.

"You can't do this to your own daughter!" I shouted after him.

"You're right. There is no way I could ever sacrifice my own flesh and blood."

I let out the breath I was holding, waiting for him to reveal how he'd tricked the king of the underworld, the elaborate ruse of how he *hadn't* double-crossed me.

He shrugged. "But you are not my daughter."

"I'm not sure when I knew. Or maybe I always knew. But she loved me enough to lock me safe high in a tower. Even if she didn't give birth to me, Mother knows best."

—*Rapunzel Lets Down Her Hair: Unauthorized Biography*

32

Child of the Trees

The room spun. No, the entire *world* flipped upside down. *I am a child of the trees, though the wind may howl. I cannot break. I will not break. Grimm, do not let me break.*

"I know. I was disappointed too." Dad, er, Robin settled down in a chair, resting his chin on the hilt of the sword. "That whole Maid Marion story I told you." He held up his thumb and finger a little ways apart. "May have been a teensy tall tale. Marion was just a fling. She liked the fame that came with being associated with an outlaw, but when it came down to it, she wanted no part of the forest. She had me chased out of Richard's court for borrowing a small trinket, and when I got back to the woods, I found you." He slapped his knee.

"Even then, you had a big mouth. You were tucked so deep inside that ironwood's trunk, I would have walked right by you if I hadn't heard your squalling."

He jumped up, hefting the sword over his head. "Just imagine that though. An infant somehow surviving on her own, in the heart of Camlan, the great tree, sucking on glowing sap." His face lit up. "Boy, I thought I'd made the score of a lifetime." When he looked down at me, the grin was gone, replaced by hard set lines. "You were supposed to be magical. So I made up a name for you, and I put all that time and effort into feeding you, training you, telling you stories, expecting that one day that investment was gonna pay off big." He shook his head. "And you fooled me. Twice. What a waste."

"I-I don't understand."

"I'll spell it out. Sure, you glowed a bit as a baby, but you never developed a talent. There's nothing special about you. Not one remarkable attribute. I figured that out while you were a kid, bringing me useless pots and thing. So I traded you off to that Emerald witch as a tax payment. I'd written you off, but when you came back to the forest and couldn't die…" He whistled. "Man, I thought I'd hit the bull's-eye again. Marked by the empress. Marked by the King of the Underworld. Marked by the Girl of Emerald. You were my ultimate way into the easy life. But look at you now. You couldn't even hit a target that was right in front of you. You had a place at the Lady of the Lake's right hand and screwed it all up. Here I thought you were destined for greatness. Turns out you were destined to fail."

Any fight I had left in me fled.

The hero of the Sherwood Forest tied Excalibur and my boots to his back and perched on the window ledge. "In the end, you were useful twice, so I guess you weren't a total loss." Before he jumped out, he looked over his shoulder. "No hard feelings, eh, kiddo?"

Oh, there were feelings. I held them in until he was out of sight. Then I let my emotions seep out of every pore. I mourned the loss of Kato. I mourned the loss of the family I'd thought I had. I mourned the lie of the girl I'd thought I was. Not Rexi Hood, Princess of Thieves. Or Rexi of Emerald, or even Rex the Huntsman. I was nobody.

Something between a laugh and a sob escaped my lips as I realized the truth had been in front of me the whole time. "No wonder the *Compendium of Storybook Characters* didn't recognize my name. I don't have one. Morte was right. Except, instead of being born to be Forgotten, I was forgotten the moment I was born."

"I'll certainly remember ye." Mordred swung in through the open hole in the roof, agilely landing on a rafter, and front-flipped down. "That stuff that I said about you having more bark than bite…" He held up his bloody hand.

"Hex," I groaned, hiding my face. "Can't you just let me die? Go after your sword. I don't have it anymore."

"I know. I saw." Mordred bent down next to me. "Giving

up, are ye?" He scratched the stubble on his chin and crinkled his brow. "I had you pegged for someone who could take a bit more of a hit than that."

"Are you counting all the times that you've threatened to kill me?"

"Aye. And yet you are still here. And you have two legs." He poked at them with his toe. "Though a wee on the blackened side. You should get up and use them."

"What do you know?" I said and rolled over.

"I know that we don't get to pick the folk that raise us." He turned my face until I had to meet his ember eyes. "But we *do* get to pick those we call family."

I thought of Dorthea and Kato, Hydra and Verte… They were my family.

"Don't they be needing ye to save the day?"

I narrowed my eyes. "Really? That's what you're going with? A pep talk? Your manipulation skills suck."

His lip curled. "Last part a wee much? I was thinking of going with 'what doesn't kill you only maims you a bit.'"

"We just watched Excalibur get walked out of here, and you are trying to cheer me up with rotted clichés. Just because I'm mostly dead doesn't mean I'm brain dead. What do you want from me?"

Mordred threw back his head and laughed. "I had to try. You have proven yourself my equal at most every turn, so I shall deal with you as such. For me, the beginning and end has always been the grail. After listening to your conversations now and back at the library, 'tis my belief that thou art my best chance at finding it. Plus, you amuse me, so I'd prefer you not to perish. However, I admit I care naught for your friends' welfare. The beasts dragged thine friend onto the shore, but she is fading. I would be willing to use the grail to save her before I go about mine business. Or I could use it to free thee from all those marks the thief spoke of, whichever you desire; it matters naught to me. Just deliver me the grail."

I had been betrayed, tricked, used, or abandoned by just about everyone, so I had no reason to believe anything Mordred said. Except he *did* seem to be right about one thing—the power drain had slowed, so Dorthea wasn't in the water anymore. She was so weak, I could hardly feel her presence. Which I might not have minded if that didn't mean she was near dying. And taking me with her.

I sighed. "Of course, it has to be one or the other, save Dorthea or release me. It can't be both."

"Aye. Would you prefer I lie to you and promise thee eternal life and that we shall share the grail? I am being honorable in my frankness. I am not a hero whose actions come out of the kindness of my withered heart. If you show me the grail, you may use it but once."

"And if I say sod off?"

He clapped his knees and stood up. "Then thy life, or what might be left of it, is thine own. 'Tis no skin off my elbow. I'll find the man pretending to be Merlin and offer him the same."

I considered his offer. At this point, I really didn't have anything to lose. Mordred was unapologetically exactly who he was, neither sinner nor savior. Or perhaps a little of both. Aside from misquoting lingo, he meant what he said and followed through, which was a far cry better than most. There was just one problem: I knew Blanc had the grail, but she could have left it at the Academy of Villains with the other magical artifacts, or it could be in the lake. And if she was carrying it, then we were going to need everyone in Story to take it off her.

"All right," I agreed. "I don't know exactly where the grail is though."

Mordred's eyes darkened nearly as black as his hair. "Then you cannot help me."

"Wait! I know that the Lady of the Lake has it."

"I had guessed as much." He knelt down and scooped me into his arms, hoisting me over his shoulder like a sack of flour. "For confirming that, I suppose I can deposit you into a chair. Hopefully that Merlin imposter knows better."

The idea of Mic getting the grail soured my stomach.

When Mordred tried to set me down on Gwennie's office chair, I kicked and squirmed until he let go of my legs enough that I could wrap and lock them around his waist.

He shook his head. "What is it with you? Art thou a monkey?"

"No, but I'm going to hang on until you listen to me."

"Fine, hang on as long as you can," he said and turned, walking out of the model castle. "You'll make an excellent shield or bait for the night mares when ye lose your grip."

He'd let go of me entirely, so I was hanging on with whatever strength I had left. "Look, I can still be helpful. I've spent some time in the lake, but I've never seen the grail. Or any cup for that matter."

"Common myth conception," he said. "Despite legends pertaining to the fountain of youth, the grail is not something as powerless as a cup."

"What is it then?"

"'Tis not the container that has power but the contents. And the lifeblood of any story will always be its ink."

"The grail is an inkwell!" I gasped and smacked Mordred on the back, grateful that I still had that memory. "I know where it is!"

"*Rule #82: When you can't find the words to express your feelings, find a sunset or a lake to look forlornly at. A power ballad will smooth over that awkward moment and solve all your trust issues.*"

—*Definitive Fairy-Tale Survival Guide, Volume 1*

It Takes a Thief

Mordred slowed, stopping his jiggling to try to get me to fall off. "I practically said as much. Thou art bluffing to save your skin."

With one hand, I showed him the size of the grail, how the pewter filigree scrolled around the edges. "And the ink is clear but shimmery."

Placing his hands under my armpits, he pulled me off him and held me out to dangle at arm's length. "You have seen it truly?" When I nodded, his eyes filled and threatened to spill over. "Finally, it will be over!" He crushed me to him.

"Um, what are you doing?" I wheezed.

"A thousand pardons. Oh, bloody box it all, we don't have

time for this." With a quick shift, he cradled me in the crook of his arms, taking off at a sprint toward Avalon.

"I still wish I hadn't lost Excalibur," I said.

Mordred patted my shoulder. "'Tis all right."

I leaned back so I could get a good look at his face. He really didn't seem upset at all. "You have been very unscorched about this."

"Shall I tell you a secret?" He craned his head in close and whispered, "If you looked very closely along the blade, it was written: reproduction—Made in Nottingham."

"No hexing way!"

"Excalibur can never be tricked or gained by magic. It reveals itself when it decides it is ready for the king to return. And not a moment sooner. My wish was just a farce so all thought I had the rightful sword."

Even though it hurt, I roared with laughter. "After all that, Robin Hood ran off with a fake." I laughed so hard that tears rolled down my cheeks. Once they started, the tears turned to sobs and wouldn't stop. I was betrayed by a father I had thought loved me...all for a Nottingham pawn knockoff. The absolute ironic proof of my worthlessness finally made me snap.

Mordred shoved my face into his chest. "Please stop that. Such sadness is unbecoming of a knight in training."

"Im mrph a mrph in mrping." (I'm not a knight in training.)

"When I have the grail and Excalibur, I will need people I can trust beside me." He squeezed tighter. "I want to change the history of Mad Arthur's war, not repeat it. Camelot will be better this time. Blind ideals won't have to be paid for in…"

His jog stopped as abruptly as his words. I wiped my leaking nose on his tunic and turned to see which glittery pony was about to skewer us. Instead, I saw death.

Much like in the clearing, Dorthea lay on her back, and the land around her for at least two dozen giant's lengths was completely drained of life. The grass, brown and brittle. The flowers, wilted and dried. The trees, barren and twisted. Several small critters lay next to piles of glitter dotting the otherwise desolate circle of destruction.

Kato paced on all fours, just skirting the edge of the kill zone. When his paw got a little too close, Verte scolded him to stay clear.

Kato swiped his tail through the crumbling reeds. "This is ridiculous. She'd never hurt me."

"Maybe." Verte stepped on his tail to hold him still. "But Dot ain't really home right now. And the curse likes you just fine too, as a snack."

Mic was still in beast form and seemed to have no trouble keeping his distance from the boundary. Gwen was nowhere to be seen. Only Oz was in the circle, tending to Dorthea.

"How come the curse doesn't eat him?" I asked.

Kato perked at my voice, his muzzle turning up until he saw the condition I was in and who was holding me. He growled. "What's *he* doing?"

At the same time, Mordred asked, "What is *that*?"

"Down, boys." Verte grumbled something about needing a spray bottle or a rolled up scroll.

"Later." I waved away both their questions.

"Assuming there is a later," Mic grumbled.

"So Blanc is still…" I trailed off as Verte tossed me the charred book we'd seen on the eyepod. The title had changed to read *The Lost City of Atlantis*. Blanc's sigil, the lotus rose—water lily, whatever—was engraved on the front. An entire story vanished in the space of an hour. The book now only had one picture: Blanc sitting upon the throne among the ruins. A crown of black pearls rested on her white hair, gold circlets on her wrists and neck. She was clothed in a gown of shimmery seafoam and holding the copper trident like a scepter. An empress of an empty city.

"And what of the grail?" Mordred asked, setting me down gently.

Mic snorted. "It was all the mutt and I could do to rescue the crown princess. Between the White One's army of sea creatures and her control of the waters, she's built herself a fortress. There's no way we can penetrate it."

I turned toward the water. "I'll do it."

Kato cantered over, towering above me. "Whatever you are scheming, the answer is no."

"You really are bossy." I flicked his muzzle. "I know where the grail is. I'm going to go bring it back here."

"*We're* going to bring it back here," Mordred corrected.

"Over my dead body," Kato growled.

Mordred put his hand on the ax at his side. "Easily arranged. Your head would be a prize for any hunter's wall."

"Did you miss the part where, in my magnificence, I asserted that the defenses were impenetrable?" Mic called over the posturing.

"All of you shut up!" I said. "Tell me if I'm missing something. Blanc is gonna get her binds off any minute, Dorthea's the only who can stop her, but if we don't cure the madness of the curse, then we have to worry about both the flood and the fire."

"I can keep her in check," Kato muttered, but I don't think even he believed the words as he said them.

Verte repeated the prophecy everyone knew by heart now. "Girl of Emerald, no man can tame. Burn down the world, consumed by flames."

The shores of Camelot were eerily quiet.

"Let us go," Mordred said, walking toward the water.

I grabbed the back of his shirt. "I have to go alone."

That didn't sit well with anyone. Mic, Verte, Kato, and Mordred all yelled their arguments at once, making it impossible to hear any of them. Safe to say it was all a resounding *no*.

"Look, I'm not trying to be a hero. And I'm not trying to cheat or betray anyone. Mic said it: none of you can get past the lake's defenses or know the way to Avalon."

Then came the dreaded question I could only avoid for so long…

"And you think you can?"

I didn't look at any of them as I said, "I know I can."

The ground shook. My head snapped up as a green ele-phonkey charged toward us, spraying me down with water. With a puff it was gone and Oz stood there, holding my hand and *The Lost City of Atlantis*.

"What are you up to now, meddler?" Verte asked, wringing the drops of water off her mole.

"Wait for it," I said quietly as the water soaked into my skin, making the inked flower underneath it shimmer. The Lady of the Lake's mark. The empress's mark.

"I knew I'd remember where I'd seen that flower." Oz shrugged. "That is all." Without another word, he walked back to Dorthea and left me to sort out the mess.

Kato said only one word. "Why?" The light leaving his eyes said so much more.

"The why doesn't matter, fool." Mic grabbed my wrist and inspected it. "This is the blessing of the empress's champion. The bearer is immune to any water attacks, can breathe underwater, summon and go through the whirlpool. How she got the mark doesn't matter. Just be grateful that she does because it increases the odds of survival from zero."

"He's right," Verte said. "Ten percent now, at least."

"Great." I rolled my eyes.

I reached up to ruffle Kato's mane, but he stepped back with a wince. I understood how he felt and didn't hold it against him. Thanks to my Dorthea-bond vision, I got to see a repeat of when I handed Griz the star, except from both Dorthea's and my standpoint. I got to feel her heartbreak. Even though I was barefoot now, I understood the adage "the shoe is on the other foot." I saw both sides, hero and villain.

Let me tell you, the view sucked.

I stepped backward, keeping both Kato and Mordred in sight. "Trust me." Then I turned around before I could see if they believed me.

My shadow stretched out before me, bending away from the water, about as eager to touch it as I was.

"While I was away, you have turned into quite the little hero after all. Whoever would have guessed?"

No. I was definitely not a hero. It's not like I wanted to save the day. In fact, I would have much preferred someone else have the job. No one else could though, and I would do whatever I needed to, to save my family.

But if you asked me, a ten percent chance of survival was optimistic.

"Obsession is the hunger than gnaws your insides. And when it destroys you from the inside out, you still beg for more."

—Evil Queen, *Shattered Reflections*

Hate Is Blind

I'd never tried to get to Avalon before. I'd always either been dragged there or... Nope, only been dragged. Mic said I could summon the whirlpool. So I dove into the lake and swam down, willing the water to spin like the cyclone Dorthea and I rode out of Emerald. I imagined the whirlpool sucking me into the swirling vortex and spitting me out into the caves of Avalon. The mark on my wrist tingled and glowed, and the water obeyed.

Being in charge of the whirlpool made it a much smoother ride. I popped my head out of the water, just enough to see. It was exactly as I hoped. No one was home. Pulling myself up, I slipped out of the water and onto the rock as quietly as I could. This would be an in-and-out job. I scampered silently over to the oyster desk, then remembered what happened anytime I thought a heist would be easy in and out. Something always went wrong. In this case, the inkwell wasn't there.

No! I pushed aside scallops, and shrimps scattered, but the inkwell was nowhere to be found.

The sound of water circling made me freeze. Unsure of who it was, I ducked behind a rock formation and held my breath. The moments ticked by. Finally, there came another sound—a slurping noise.

"I know you're there."

Blanc.

She was fishing, waiting to see if I would give up my position. Well, I wasn't that—

"You're behind the limestone peak. You left inky footprints of that reaper's filth. You may as well come out."

I looked down at my feet, and the Lady of the Lake was right. No doubt Morte was upping his stain on me, trying to hasten my demise. Without the boots, this death would be my last. And the Grimm Reaper seemed to be waiting impatiently.

I stepped out from behind the rocks to see the Lady of the Lake, composed half of squid and a dozen or so snapping turtles this time.

"I thought we were friends. So why do you hide from me?" she asked.

I thought about every con that might make a convincing

story, but tact had never been my strong suit. "Let's just be straight and get it over with. You're Blanc, and I'm breaking in to steal from you. Now what?"

I don't know what I expected, but trills of laughter weren't it. "Very well," she said, and the turtles and squid dropped to the ground, slipping into the nearest pool. The White Empress rose smoothly from the waters. "It takes a surprising amount of effort to control those creatures, but I couldn't very well just show my true form from the beginning. You'd already made your mind up about me without hearing my side."

"Your *lies* you mean."

"No. Think back. I haven't told you one false statement." She gestured to the last turtle crawling away. "I apologize for the puppetry, but the rest is who I truly am. I am not like that charlatan Mimikos, pretending to be someone else. Long before I was called Blanc the White Empress, I was simply the Lady of the Lake. Some men of this land worshipped me as a goddess; others feared me as a demon siren. The rest of my family and I, all elementals, were blamed every time there was a flood, a drought, an earthquake, or a lightning strike."

She'd hit a sore spot. "Or, I don't know, steal someone's life force and hit them with stormbolts."

Blanc shrugged serenely. "And I should be judged for my sister Grizelda's actions? From the moment I entered into the world, I have been saddled with the blame for others' choices. Blamed for the stupidity of men who sacrificed their virgin daughters on my shores. Some to appease the wicked demon and protect the village. Some to garner favor and harness my powers for their own benefits."

Blanc hit the bull's-eye again, and emotional wounds Robin inflicted on me hurt anew.

"I never asked for that," Blanc said, holding her hands to her chest. "I wanted to live in a world where people were free to decide their own fates, in spite of their births. So I gave a peasant boy a sword and made him a king, not the knight who was supposed to have it. I changed the story. I thought I controlled my own destiny. I was wrong. And I paid the price."

Listening to her, it really was hard to remember that she was the enemy. She was a victim. She'd lost the one she loved and had to watch him die. Blanc had had everything taken from her.

"I can tell what you're thinking," she said. "I already told you that we are much too alike for my own good. Which is why you wear my blessing and why I'm not going to kill you for trying to steal the grail."

"You're not?" I coughed. "I mean, grail? What grail? I was just gonna steal the trident since Excalibur was a bust."

"Now who's lying?" She motioned with her hand, her fingers making the water dance, parting it until I could see the grail. "This is what you're after so you can save that destroyer."

I snorted. "Hypocrite much? You took out an entire story just a minute ago."

"They're casualties of war. Sacrifices have to be made if we are going to fix the system." She walked toward me with her arms open. "I can't do it alone. Help me create a new world where there are no more children abandoned in trees. No more needless suffering just to make sure some insipid princess gets her happy ever after."

The passion in her eyes and the empathy in her voice cooled some of the anger in my soul. Whatever Oz said, I didn't believe that Blanc was down-to-the-bone evil. She wasn't mean, nasty, and cruel simply to get power and make herself happy. And the Storymaker system sucked. Gods creating characters to amuse them and dance to their tunes. But that didn't mean what Blanc was doing was right.

Oh, and she was absolutely nuts.

There was no universe where it made sense to sacrifice thousands, to cause pain in order to spare people from pain. In trying to give characters a choice and a chance at controlling their own fates, Blanc had taken away their futures. Trying to make sense of it all made my head hurt.

And that whole ten percent survival was getting slimmer by the second. I had one chance. I was going to have to be fast. There were really good odds I wasn't going to survive it in the end.

I let Blanc embrace me, and behind her back, I waved at DumBeau. *Help me*, I mouthed. He nodded, not nearly as dumb as all of us thought him to be. I pointed to the grail on the ground and hoped he understood.

Not wanting to seem off, I pulled back. "I wish I could help you. I do. But as you can see, Morte is going to claim me as soon as Dorthea loses it again."

Blanc traced a line down my face, looking into my eyes. "I can protect you from both, but I need these binds off first." She held out her wrists. "If you free me, I will free you."

DumBeau was moving behind her, and she would notice as he got close. I would have to play along, just long enough. The timing would have to be perfect.

"Tell me what to do."

She narrowed her eyes but nodded. "The trident. Someone else has to willingly hold it and choose to release my binds." Holding on to the tip of the trident with one hand, she pressed under the bracelet with the other. "Grab on to the end and say *Libération*."

I nodded. *Hurry up*, I pleaded to DumBeau.

"Well, go on."

Forgive me, I thought, then said, "*Libération*." The left bracelet crumbled to dust. Miniwaves rose out of the pools. A new rush of heat filled my wrist, and the lotus rose sigil glowed anew.

Blanc's smile was brilliant as she closed her eyes and said, "Yessss."

She let go of the trident, so I could shift it to the other wrist.

"*Liber*... Now!" I yelled at DumBeau. He tossed the grail to me and wrapped his arms around Blanc, holding her tight.

He smiled. "Good-bye, Rex."

Grail in one hand, trident in the other, I jumped into the pool and willed myself to Camelot. I waited for the whirlpool to choke me, pull me back, but it spit me out on the shore.

"Thank you," I whispered to the only person who had never once asked anything from me. I hoped DumBeau would be okay but knew he wouldn't be able to hold her long.

Kato held vigil near the shore, at the edge of the circle of dead grass. It had grown larger, and unconscious Dorthea was still being held by Oz's and Verte's magic. Hydra was back, without the nose clamp and accompanied by an army of fiery, pink and purple unicorns. So, not Hydra. Gwenevere.

Mordred ran toward me. "Do you have it?"

"Run!" was all I had time to say before the lake exploded behind me.

"Too late." Blanc grabbed my ankle and started dragging me back. "Kill them all," she commanded an army of hammerheads, crocodiles, and other water creatures that had risen from the depths at Blanc's command.

Kato soared over and ripped me out of her grasp. He deposited me in Mordred's arms. "Get her out of here."

Mordred nodded and ran away from the chaos.

"Hey, put me down. We have to help." I kicked and fought. "Coward."

"You may pay for that name-calling later, but for now you have to get out of the way and let them fight without worrying about your safety."

As he ran, I could see the battle over his shoulder. Verte and

Oz put up a shield around Dorthea. Kato and Mic used their might as chimeras to pick off every creature that came for them. I expected Blanc to charge toward me, but something caught her attention. Something she wanted even more than the grail, me, or Dorthea. She spotted Gwen.

Blanc raised her hand and brought a massive tsunami up from the lake and down on the shore. Dorthea was protected in her force field, but the rest of us got drenched. Including the night mares. Fires out, the unicorns abandoned their mistress.

Blanc hadn't taken a step out of the water before Gwen was on the hill. I knew what the water witch had planned when I saw her pull out the spark of gold.

"Gwen's going to die and Hydra with her," I said with absolute certainty. After grabbing Mordred's hand, I shoved the inkwell in it. "Keep your promise."

"Aye, but what are you going to do?" he asked, but I was already running full tilt with the trident in my hand.

Blanc twisted her hands, and water flowed from the lake, forming a bow with a strand of kelp. As soon as she fired, I hit Blanc's arrow using the trident like a bat, but the arrow curved and corrected course. The magical golden arrow had perfect aim, and Blanc's obsession with Gwen was written on her face. If she saw me running at her with the trident, she didn't flinch.

"It's all you," Kato yelled as I ran past. The air turned frigid, and the water around Blanc turned to ice, freezing her in place.

As I reached into my pocket, I briefly wondered if Kato would have helped me if he knew what I was about to do.

With a final burst of speed, I ran Blanc through with the trident. When her mouth opened in surprise, I shoved in the pearl just before her arrow struck Gwen.

It wasn't the way the pearl was intended to be used, but Blanc's eyes grew wide as the magic did its work. The wheels of time ground to a halt. Even the breeze seemed to hold its breath. Then the arrow spun around as Blanc forgot everyone except who was right in front of her—me.

A sense of déjà vu struck me along with the arrow in my back. I guess, some things are just destined to be, no matter how you try to change them. When I died the first time from Griz's stormbolt in the back, I should have stayed dead. Except Dorthea became the Storymaker and changed the ending I'd been written. With my shadow growing, I knew my end was out of her hands this time.

"*A willing sacrifice. The final piece I needed to rise again. I'm growing impatient, so while your body dies, I'm afraid I'm reclaiming your soul for some unfinished business with me.*"

My world turned to shades of gray as I fell to the sand, blood and shadow spreading out beneath me and swallowing me whole.

I'll Follow You Down

The landscape of Nome Ore that used to rise and fall was now barren and flat. Empty. All that remained was the forge and ink pit. The wails of Forgotten were eerily absent. Tragic that even their last protests were taken from them.

Mine were as well. My shadow was now completely controlled by Morte, corporeal and restraining—inky tar oozing over my mouth and nose and every inch of me. As if that torture was incomplete, Griz slithered back and forth over me, creating snake tracks.

I have been waiting for thissss.

Entombed in tar, maybe I couldn't go kicking and

screaming into the dark night, but Morte had left my eyes uncovered. And I could glare with the best of them.

"Oh, don't give me that look," Morte said. "I'm giving you exactly what you wanted. To be special." He pulled my mangled and melted plotline out of his suit pocket. It was no longer straight and knotted. Some parts were thick and braided with green-oxidized wire, while other parts where so thin and withered the wire looked like it would snap. "You are my masterpiece. Every death, every piece of magic thrust on you and in you has honed your meat sack into a suitable host for me. You chose this as much as I did." He then ran his scythe along my cheekbone. Griz ran her forked tongue along the other. "I'm going to take my time and enjoy this," he said as he pressed the line against my neck.

"Sorry," a voice said, filling the empty air. "I came as fast as I could."

Kato.

Somehow, he'd come for me. My soul felt light, and the tar grew less sticky, sliding off me.

Morte eased off some of the pressure and looked up. "I'm sorry, but the office of death will be closed indefinitely, so I'm afraid you'll have to help yourself." He turned his other-worldly, white eyes to me, squinting at the ink sloughing off my skin. He looked at Kato again and threw his head back with a guttural sound. "No. I forbid it! You can't bring her back to life again. I've spent far too long preparing this girl. She chose to die; that makes her mine."

"That's where you are wrong. I didn't have to bring her back to life because, technically, I got to her before her heart stopped beating," Kato said, stepping close enough for me to see his front paws muted and gray. And not a claw left on either of them.

"What have you done?" Morte released me and stalked over to Kato.

The rest of the tar slid off me, my soul growing lighter to the point of turning to mist. Griz fell right through me as I began to rise. "Nonononononono," I bellowed as I clawed and flailed, trying to hold on to something. I reached for Kato, but my hand slipped through him.

Kato looked up at me and smiled. "May your embers burn ever bright, hearth sister."

"No! I didn't ask you to trade places with me." As I floated farther away, I stared at the last nail that he sacrificed to make my heart keep beating, knowing it would silence his. "Oh Grimm, why?"

The shadows lurched at Kato, encircling his muzzle to keep him from speaking. The warmth in his wintery-blue eyes was the only answer I would ever have as inky tendrils swirled and pulled his body to the ground, covering him like a death shroud. Kato's gaze stayed locked with mine until the last moment.

As I faded away from the underworld, I relived one of Dorthea's memories. A dream she'd told me about. Except some of the details were different.

I stared into the mirror. Dorthea stared back at me. She looked sickly pale, hair falling out in patches, and she was dressed in a long, white robe. She held a leather-bound book with gold leafing. After opening the book, she ripped out a page.

Before I could grab it, the wind kicked up and stole the page from my fingertips.

I chased after it and screamed my frustration into the sky.

The sky screamed back.

Kato crested the hill of wildflowers, but he wasn't the kind-eyed chimera anymore. He was a black beast that could have swallowed Sherwood Forest whole. He reared back and roared again.

The trees shook in fear.

As my soul snapped back into my body, the vision shifted to reality.

A roar shook the very ground beneath me. I scrambled and clawed clear of the stain my shadow had left behind in the sand. I bumped into Blanc's feet. The ice Kato had magically trapped her with had melted, so she stood in a small puddle, tinged red from the blood dripping from the wound I'd given her.

"Congratulations," she said, ripping the trident out of her side. "It seems he loved you after all." With a flick of her finger, Blanc called forth a riptide, dragging me back into the water. I searched the hills for help, but all my friends were lying on the ground inside the circle of dead grass. Unconscious or, worse, drained from the curse. Blanc's creatures were scattered around the shore as well as some of the other patients from the institute, who had come out to see what was going on.

They were all in danger. Morte was coming. I called out to warn them, but my screams were garbled by the waters that closed around me. I couldn't drown, but the liquid held me like a prison.

A twin-tailed black chimera burst from the ground and into the air. His eyes and horns were white. He had no claws. "The king has returned." Morte's voice overlaid Kato's in soul-shattering discord.

"Don't put off tomorrow what you can do today. There's no better way to put a cramp in your inevitable domination than to leave an archnemesis around to witness it."

—Seven Habits of Highly Evil People

Aim True

"Y̲ou finally found a way out. Don't get used to it. I haven't forgiven you for keeping my sister trapped in the underworld." Blanc held one arm at her side and raised the trident in the other. Water columns shot into the air, wrapping around Morte's wings, pulling him to the ground.

I wondered why Blanc didn't just suck the life out of him, but she looked as if she was having trouble breathing herself. The gold collar around her neck tightened as she drew on its power. She dropped the trident and clawed at her neck. The water lost shape and began falling like rain.

"With most of your power still bound, we are at an impasse, so I offer you a truce." Morte's dark, smooth voice came out of

Kato's mouth. His pupils were white. It was Kato's body, but it wasn't Kato anymore. Only the Grimm Reaper. "Grizelda's soul was so shattered by the disenchantment the Girl of Emerald used that this"—he waved one of his tails, not Kato's dragon-scale tail, but the other twin tail that Morte had added, an enormous silver snake, snapping and hissing wildly—"was the only life I could offer your sister. I saved her from the ink forge and brought her with me as an offering. To you."

He circled around Blanc, letting the snake caress her cheek as he spoke in low, sultry tones. "Excalibur will soon be in my possession. Agree to rule with me, Blanc, I will free your binds and use my ink to turn this story's useless characters into an army of shadow souls to do our bidding."

My core shook as I pictured a living army of Forgotten at Blanc's and Morte's command. If the two joined forces, the world of Story would fall into a darkness that would make Nome Ore look like a cuddly enchanted forest. I argued helplessly, unheard, for Blanc not to listen to him, that his sword was a fake. Except Blanc didn't need my help to decide what to do with Morte.

She reached slowly to the shadow chimera to caress his face in return. "Never. I serve no one. I need no one." With a snap, she yanked his muzzle down, put her lips to his, and breathed in. Dark life flowed from Morte into Blanc, the water beneath her feet turning black.

I felt Dorthea regain consciousness at the same time I heard her.

"Kato!" The *O* dragged out into a wail filled with so much raw emotion it not only pierced my ears, but it also pierced my heart. It was the sound of someone's soul shattering. I knew, because that's the exact sound I would have made if I could have. I mourned Kato's choice doubly—for myself and for the pieces of Dorthea that lived within me.

Dorthea's cry made the water sorceress aware she had an audience. Blanc stalled her death kiss for a moment to sneer at Dorthea's pain. "I watched helpless from my cell as you murdered my only family," Blanc said. "Now I will return the favor."

Let it burn. Take it all. Make them bend.

The twisted chorus of voices in my mind was my only warning before Dorthea's entire body erupted into flames.

A phoenix would have looked like a single match compared to the blinding, green bonfire before me.

"Give him back," Dorthea cried in a voice not her own. Half-mad but all fury, she flicked her arm and a torrent of flames headed for Blanc.

The elemental witch raised her hands, the water coming to her aid and canceling out Dorthea's Emerald fire.

Blanc's neck wrinkled as the choker did its job, cutting off her air supply.

"Care to reconsider my offer?" Morte asked. He stood up, but his legs wobbled from the drain.

Blanc's pale face was turning blue, so she only nodded. Morte threw his body, Kato's body, in between Blanc and Dorthea.

"Dot, please. I love you. Save me," the black chimera said as the flames scorched his dragon's tail.

Dorthea clenched her fist, sealing the flame. I cried and cursed from my water prison, but she couldn't hear me. She only saw what she wanted to see: a glimmer of the real Kato. She ignored the empty gaze and the discordant voice because the words were what Dorthea wanted. She was so blinded by that, that she didn't see the silver snake tail striking until it knocked her across the field.

My watery prison burst as Blanc grabbed the trident and focused all her powers on Dorthea. "Finish her!" Blanc ordered her new ally.

Morte tsked derisively. "Your centuries locked away have not improved your temperament. Just as in the time of Lancelot and Arthur, your actions are ruled by emotion. And that will be your downfall. Behold, the Girl of Emerald."

Dorthea's flames shot into the air, filling the sky like green, thunderous clouds—all while she was still unconscious. The other villains who had been watching the fight from the hill scattered and searched for cover.

"Without your full powers, defeating her at the height of her madness is dangerous and near impossible. Let us go and watch from a safe distance as the child destroys herself and all she loves. Surely that will satisfy your thirst for revenge." Morte swept his tail under Blanc and placed her on his back, ignoring her protests. "I will see you again, little hero. You are not free of me yet," he said to me before flying away with his empress.

Dorthea bolted upright. She opened her eyes, her stare blank and green.

We need power to take him back.

It was the curse chorus, but this time it came out of Dorthea's mouth. She shoved her hands into the dirt. For a moment, nothing happened. Then lines of fire surged along the ground, like a forest python weaving back and forth, hunting for prey. Everywhere the fire touched turned brown and lifeless. Everything it touched was sucked dry. *Everyone* it touched…

The first to feel Dorthea's fire were the troll brothers climbing under the bridge for cover. The power reached for a nearby tree but found a tastier snack. The trolls brayed as they burned. As their shrieks died down, their voices joined the chorus.

More. More like that.

Other villains I'd met at the institute panicked and ran in every direction. But the Emerald curse hunted them down. Some of Blanc's creatures remained, fighting and picking off the weakened.

"Stop!" Verte called, jamming her staff into the ground. Dorthea's flames dimmed and flickered. "You must control the curse, not the other way around. I will not allow you to destroy yourself and the world along with you."

Dorthea tilted her head, like she was listening. The flames momentarily stopped pursuing the fleeing villains.

"*Feed us,*" Dorthea said in the curse's chorus. As she twisted her hands, every tendril of flame aimed for Verte.

"No!" I cried, warning Verte.

She looked at me and nodded. Her emerald belt winked as the flames covered it.

I closed my eyes. I couldn't watch.

Now, the chorus said. My eyes snapped open at the sound. A new voice had taken the lead. Verte's.

Dorthea stood rigid, her arms flung wide, creating an arc of fire that left me untouched. Her face was lined with bulging veins of green, but her eyes—they were normal. And they stared at me, wide with a look that wrenched at my heart and spoke volumes of horror and agony through our bond. Her mouth said only one thing: "Kill me."

I shook, my body rejecting the request. There was no way. As tight as the connection was now, we were practically the same person. Stopping Dorthea would mean sacrificing myself too. And Kato would have died for nothing. And there would be no one left to stop Blanc and Morte.

The brief respite in Dorthea's storm passed as her eyes shifted green again and the arc of power ensnared me. The curse again tore away at my life and my sanity. *This is how it ends,* I despaired. *Not with a scream but with the whispering of a thousand voices. Calling for me to join them.*

All is one and one is all.

Join us. Feed us.

Bring us more.

There is no hope. No savior. No end.

"*No time to waste!*" Verte's voice shouted, taking the dominant position in the chorus. "*You must free her. Break the curse.*"

"How?" I struggled to answer. "I have no magic, no sword. I am not hero. I am just me."

"How do you know you aren't enough?" Verte said, her voice blowing through me and waning like the tail end of a forest breeze. Then her presence was gone.

Mordred charged at Dorthea but was knocked back by a flaming shield Dorthea crafted twisting just her fingers.

"That will not work, fool," Oz chided, wrapping his arms around Dorthea from behind. He was unaffected by the curse but struggled to hold her in place. "Only the grail can save her now. The ink is thicker than blood, as the pen is mightier than the sword."

"It is hopeless," Mordred moaned, holding a melted ax in one hand and the grail in the other. "I cannot..."

Girl of Emerald, no man can tame, the curse taunted.

Well, I was not a man. And I had an idea.

"Be true to your word," I called to Mordred and held my hand out for the grail. He hesitated only the barest of seconds, which was good because Oz could only keep the curse's attention off me for so long.

The ink needed to get inside Dorthea's bloodstream to break the curse. But I doubted she was just gonna let me run up and pour it in a cut.

After pulling the pen out of my pocket, I sucked the ink up inside it and looked around for something to fire my makeshift arrow with. I only had me. And me would have to be enough. With my left wrist burning with Blanc's mark,

I called for the water. With my right hand, I pulled some of the green flame. I focused my mind and willed the elements together, like I'd seen both Blanc and Dorthea do. I molded them into the shape of a crossbow. Though I longed for the golden crossbow because my aim sucked, the borrowed magic was the best I could do.

I closed my eyes to block out the people screaming and fighting one another, settling old scores or perhaps taking sides with Blanc—who knew. Ignoring the chaos around me, I heard Verte's parting words from the clearing. "*Be yourself. Ink is thicker than blood. Aim true.*" Opening my eyes again, I let the pen fly loose toward its target. Dorthea.

The pen cut through the distance between us in less time than it takes for a grain of sand to fall. Like a bull's-eye, the sharpened tip pierced through the opal resting on Dorthea's chest. The air thickened, and time seemed to slow as the green in the opal receded, leaving the gemstone dark and empty.

A shockwave threw me to the ground, and time seemed to stop. There was not a sound in all the world. My life had been held inside that stone for long, and I broke it. I waited to die. Yet I felt more alive than ever—felt more myself. I felt for the bond. It wasn't there. All my memories of the Emerald Palace were through my eyes, not that of a princess. I had a sudden disdain for all footwear. When I thought of Kato, I still loved him, yet not with the same breathless abandon. His loss no longer destroyed me, just maimed—and made me determined to kick Morte out and bring Kato back.

The fight with the curse was over. We had won.

With a loud gasp and frenzy of sound, time resumed its pace. I could move again.

"We did it!" I cried, sitting up, excited to see Dorthea without the cursed green in her eyes or her flaming hair.

Dorthea looked like I remembered her growing up, regular hazel eyes and silky, chestnut hair. Except those locks were splayed around her unmoving body. And a silver-and-sapphire-hilted sword pierced through her chest, pinning her to the ground.

"Rule #999: Happily Ever After begins after the villain is defeated, the prince and princess kiss, and the kingdom rejoices. The End."

—*Definitive Fairy-Tale Survival Guide, Volume 1*

37

Once and Future King

My feet wouldn't move. My brain refused to believe. My eyes could not block out the truth.

What had I done?

Dorthea lay on the rocky ground, skewered through the chest by a sword—like a flutterbye to a mat. After turning her head slightly, she looked me in the eye. Her mouth moved, but only a gurgling sound came out. Then a cough racked her body, staining her lips red.

The contrast of the blood against her pale skin made my actions real. I ran to her side.

"I'm sorry. Oh Grimm, forgive me. Hang on." I held Dorthea's hand and frantically looked around for Oz. "Help her!" I screamed. Oz stayed where he was, solemnly clasping his hands with a slight nod of his head.

I was about to hurl curses at him when a spark of green wafted in front of my face. Like a will-o'-the-wisp. Then another. I gazed back down at Dorthea, her body slowly breaking up into the green embers.

"Nonononono! You can't leave me too. This is not what I wanted."

Dorthea squeezed my hand, the madness no longer twisting the veins across her face as her lips formed two words before flaking off into green ash.

Thank. You.

And then she was gone. The sword still pierced the ground, but I was left holding empty air as the green embers spiraled upward and floated away.

Chaos still reigned around me on the battleground. The fleeing. The fighting. The fallen.

My hand was on the hilt of the sword before I could think through my actions. I ripped the sword from the shale and laid the blade flat against Oz's bare throat.

"You knew that would happen." It wasn't a question.

"It was the only way. For the story to progress, she needed to—"

"Die?" I rotated the blade, scraping the skin under his chin. "Bring her back."

"I don't have that power. And even if I did, Dorthea is exactly where she needs to be. As are you."

Our scene was drawing in some of the surviving villains and orderlies from the institute, but I didn't care. The sword gleamed, bright with my fury and pain.

"You think you get to decide our fates? What…" I tried to catch my breath and stop the sobs from rising up my throat. "What…gives…you…the right? We are free…to choose."

"Never has that been more true. I can't wait to see how this story turns out." Taking a step back, he put a hand to his chest, then kneeled.

As he kneeled before me, I could see the rest of the field around me. Like trees bending to the storm, the orderlies all fell to one knee. Some villains pointed while the most notorious of them glared, their stares sharp as any blade. A murmur of whispers grew into a dull roar. I spotted Hydra and Mordred, the only two who moved toward me.

"Excalibur has been reforged." Mordred's eyes flared as he glanced at the sword that should've been his by right.

I looked at the sword in my hand, which used to be a quill.

The pen is mightier than the sword indeed. I mentally cursed the Storymaker, who merely shrugged before vanishing in a puff of smoke and the scampering of rodent feet.

"The once and future king has appeared to lead us through these dark times," Hydra said, her voice high and lofty. Regal. Gwenevere. As she and Mordred navigated their way through the crowd—villains, creatures, even Mic—fell to one knee in a motion like a wave. Crashing down on me. Threatening to drown me.

The sword in my hand grew heavy, its true weight and burden revealed.

"I'm not—"

Gwen cut me off. "All hail the return of the king!"

The crowd rose to their feet in one motion, crying, "Huzzah!"

I ignored them, rushing to Mordred. "Take it. Please take it. I don't want it."

He stared at me, considering all I offered. Reaching out, Mordred's hand shook, but pulled back before touching Excalibur. "Which is exactly why the sword and its responsibility should be in your possession."

"All I want is to bring back Dorthea and Kato! That's it. I can't lead these people."

Gwenevere closed her eyes and shook her head fiercely. "Then the story ends here. Run and we all die." When she opened her eyes again, they were each a different shade. "Fight and only most will."

I rubbed my forehead. "Thanks for that."

"You won't be alone, Rex," Mordred said. "But a ruler must always stand apart. It is a heavy burden, and only you can decide if you have the strength to bear it." He looked at me, assessing. Weighing if I had what it took.

I wish I knew.

The cheering had died down while the crowd waited for me to say something. Rot if I knew what. But the expression on most of their faces shook me to my core: hope.

What do I do?

Wanted

A lone green ember wafted on the breeze.

I raised the glowing sword to the sky and prayed to that single spark that I wouldn't screw up too badly.

The crowd broke into wild cheers of "Long live the king!"

For my part, I only wanted to hurk.

Mordred took my hand and lowered to one knee. "I will stay by your side and ensure the weight of Excalibur does not overtake you as it did Arthur. Child of the trees, my life is yours. As long as you deserve it." Looking up with a wry grin, he whispered amidst the other cheers, a message meant for only me: "Long live the queen."

The End: th-uh /'end/ *n.* the cessation of a story's narrative; a conclusion, which is really just a different sort of beginning.

—*Charlotte Webster's Dictionary of Fairy-Tale Terms*

The long-term care wing of Kansas General was normally the quietest of the entire hospital.

Not today.

A veritable army dressed in white coats and orthopedic shoes rushed back and forth through the corridors, all thanks to the coma patient in 17E who had just woken up.

"Miss…miss. I need you to calm down," the nurse explained, quickly glancing to the door, hoping that the med cart would arrive soon.

The girl in the bed ignored the caregiver and yanked the oxygen tubes from her nose. "Where am I? What's going on?"

A knock sounded on the door. A doctor strolled into the room with a chart in one hand and his other hand behind his back. "Well, hello, Miss Gayle. So nice to see you finally awake."

The girl gasped and put both hands on her chest. She looked down at her bare feet. "They're gone." She groaned.

"I think you're confused. You've been unconscious for a

long time. Let me give you a little something to help calm your nerves." The doctor swiftly pulled the syringe from behind his back and stuck it into the IV tube.

The patient clawed at the needle in her arm before the orderlies restrained her. "No, you don't understand. I have to go back. I don't belong here. People need me. I have to save him!"

Looking around the room frantically, the patient searched for a pen and paper.

There was a commotion at the door. A nurse was unsuccessfully trying to keep two people from coming into the room. "I'm sorry, but you can't be in there right now," she said.

"My daughter is in there. You and what army are going to keep me out?" a woman said in a steely tone.

The patient stopped fighting and stared at the middle-aged man and woman who pushed into the room.

"Mom! Dad!" Tears rolled freely down the girl's cheeks.

"Hi, princess," Henry Gayle said and kissed his daughter's hand. "Long time no see."

Then the sedatives took effect, and the world of Rexi, Kato, and the Storymakers became a blur in Dorothy Gayle's mind.

Acknowledgments

I have to bow down and give eternal thanks to Natalie and the Dalleys, Leslie, Kiara, Phil, Dianne, and my parents, who took turns keeping my kiddos safe and out of my hair so I could wage the never-ending fight with deadlines. I also want to thank my creative crew—Jess, Karen, TJ, Chris, Misty, Phaedra, and Joe—for their ideas and support, telling me when I suck occasionally and reminding me to be myself despite that. Things really went off the rails this year in my life, and I am grateful for the support of my agent, Michelle Witte, and my editor, Annette Pollert-Morgan, and everyone at Sourcebooks for yanking me out of the shadows and giving me the support and space I needed to make this story what it needed to be. Jeff Savage, Jen Nielsen, and slews of other word wizards—your encouragement means everything. And as always, for my family, for putting up with all the voices in my head that compete for my time. I love you all.

There's no place
like home, and
no way in spell
to get back…

Read on for a sneak peek of

Banished

"Rule #91: Once the villain is vanquished, they are gone and never coming back to get you. So stop looking over your shoulder, and think happy thoughts!"

—*Definitive Fairy-Tale Survival Guide, Volume 1*

"*This is going to pinch a little, Dorothy dear.*" Lies, I thought as the nurse shoved the needle into my hand. For once, I wanted someone to just tell me the truth. This is going to hurt. The cure sucks and may kill you faster than the cancer. But, hey, if you survive, bald is high fashion, and think of all the money you'll save on hair products.

Yeah, not a chance. The room was all decorated with upbeat cheer in mind, but I had a snarky thought pop into my brain. *Looks like a unicorn had thrown up rainbows everywhere.* Yeah that about summed it up. The pretty was all just a screen. A desperate plea to stay positive. Gotta keep your spirits up. Gotta look on the bright side. Too bad the dark side will still stab you from behind, whether you look at it or not.

Outside, the weather affirmed my opinion. I'd heard the emergency alert a half an hour ago, the siren cutting into the kids cartoons they insisted on playing. Tornado watch.

A flash of light flared into the room from the window behind me. One one thousand. Two one thousand. Three one thousand. Four one thousand. Five—

Boom.

My hand tingled and burned—a sure sign that the IV had started pumping. Liquid fire seeped through my veins. Meaning the hallucinations weren't far behind. My body felt light and my mind drifted, calling me home to the world I'd written about in my journal. A realm of Story with an Emerald palace. Where Kato was. And Rexi. Verte. Oz. A land that should be full of Happy Ever Afters, but I could already hear their screams drowning out the thunder.

It's not real, I thought. But the wails only got louder in my mind. I could picture where they were coming from. A mountain of bodies thrown into a fire pit to be melted down. My therapist said I have issues. No flippin' joke.

I focused on changing the mental picture, rewriting the story, like Dr. Baum had instructed me to do. A beach. Maybe pretend the rumbling was crashing waves. Despite my efforts, the image of the charred bodies only got stronger. I shook my head. "No it's not real. I am in control."

"You wish," a voice cackled, high pitched and off key. "Or maybe not since that's what got you into this mess."

I jerked my head around, searching the room. The monitors

beeped quicker, making music out of my racing pulse. I saw a face and opened my mouth to scream. Then realized it was the mirror. Only for a second the reflection didn't really look like me.

Nonsense. The room was empty. The only sound was the storm outside—wind howling and whipping the rain to beat against the window.

A flare of light. One one thousand. Two one thousand. Three one thousand. Four—

Crack.

Getting closer. As soon as I thought that, the electricity went out. Within seconds, the back-up generator kicked in, powering up the medical devices and emergency hallway lighting. My room remained dark except the soft glow of my monitors.

"Hello." I steadied myself on the edge of the bed, leaning out as far as the IV tether would let me. There should be nurses and doctors scrambling in the hallway. But even graveyards had more life in them than this hospital at the moment.

Where had everyone gone?

Underneath my pulse monitor's irregular percussive beep, there was another sound in the room. Drip. Drip.

It must be raining hard enough outside that the roof was leaking.

Drip. Drip.

I focused on the sound. The splash pitching deeper as the puddle grew.

The storm flashed again, lighting up the room. This time

I didn't count. I'd only had a heartbeat of illumination to see the puddle. It was black.

No. It's not real. Not real…

I grabbed the monitor and turned the screen toward the drip. The black puddle had spread, moving to the wall. And up it. Like a black figure leaning against it. I closed my eyes, telling myself the truth that it was just a shadow cast off the IV pole.

"You're being stupid. Shadows can't get you," I told myself, breathed deep, and opened my eyes again.

The shadow had moved. And it was coming closer. It oozed and grew taller, separating from the wall to walk toward me.

"Found you," the shadow gurgled. "Run."

I didn't need to be told twice. Ignoring the pain, I ripped the IV from my hand and sprinted out of the room, taking the far side from the oozing black shadows.

"Nurse! Nurse!" I yelled.

Emergency lights on the ceiling swirled, the spinning had a dizzying strobe effect. I staggered down the hall toward the illuminated exit sign. Pushing through the door, I burst onto the landing. The stairwell leading down was pitch black at the bottom. I held my breath and to hear a faint click. The sound of the emergency lights shutting off, floor by floor. Second. Then third. I was on the fifth floor. Fleeing the darkness, I headed up to the roof, taking the stairs two at a time. I hit the exit door with a thud. It wouldn't budge.

I looked over my shoulder, the lights continued to snap

off. Fourth. Fifth floor. Turning back to the exit, through the small square window at the top I could see a cyclone whipping through the city toward the hospital. A streak of lightning zig zagged down from the funnel.

The lightning was silver. And shaped like a woman.

"I told you I'd be back."

The last light in the stairwell went out, enfolding me in the darkness.

About the Author

Betsy Schow is the *Today Show*–featured author of *Finished Being Fat, Quitter's Guide to Finishing,* as well as the Storymaker's Saga: *Spelled* and *Wanted.* Her career in both fiction and nonfiction makes sense because she's been mixing up real life and fantasy for as long as she can remember. If someone were to ask about her rundown truck, she's one hundred percent positive that mechanical gremlins muck up her engine. And the only reason her house is dirty is because the dust bunnies have gone on strike. She recently moved to Maryland with her own knight in geeky armor and their two princesses (that can totally shapeshift into little beasts). When not writing, she is actively involved in Odyssey of the Mind, a program that helps teach kids to think like there is no box. Catch up and connect with Betsy at betsyschow.com.